EMILY SILVER

TRAVELIN' HOOSIER BOOKS

Cover Design by Ya'll That Graphic

Editing by Happily Editing Anns

www.authoremilysilver.com

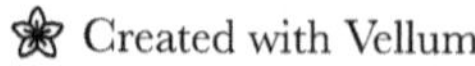 Created with Vellum

Chapter One

"**D**addy."

A finger pokes me in the side, eliciting a groan from me. Peeking one eye open, I notice that it's not even light outside.

"Daddy."

This time, her voice is a little louder.

"Daddy's still sleeping."

"How can you talk when you're sleeping?"

"Daddies are special like that."

The bed shifts beside me as Willow crawls up next to me.

"Why can't I talk when I sleep?"

"Because you aren't a grown-up."

"That stinks."

I smile, opening my eyes at my daughter. Her brown curls are an absolute mess from sleep. She's already changed into a dress-up outfit that has blue paint all over it.

Wait, blue paint?

"Willow, why is there paint on your clothes?"

"Daisy wanted to paint this morning."

"Daisy's a dog, Pipsqueak. She doesn't paint."

"She wanted to paint with me after we went swimming."

"It's too cold to go swimming."

"Nuh-uh." Willow shakes her head. "It's nice and warm in the kitchen."

My brain is tired. I was working at the bar too late and crashed the minute I got home. For a Saturday, I know it's too early to be up.

"You can't swim in the kitchen."

"Yes, I can. There's water in there."

"Since when is there water in the kitchen?"

"I dunno. It was there when Daisy and I woke up."

Oh, fuck me.

Willow hops off the bed and pads her way down to the kitchen. Grabbing the T-shirt off the end of my bed, I throw it and a pair of sweats on and follow my daughter down the hallway.

Glancing at my watch, I note it's not even six thirty yet. On a Saturday morning.

It's too fucking early to be dealing with whatever shit is waiting for me on the other side of this door.

Turning the corner into the kitchen, I find the floor covered with water.

"What the hell?"

"I told you we could swim!" Willow is bouncing up and down in the living room. It's not a huge pool of water, but enough to be a major annoyance in my day.

Wading through the puddle, I open the sink cabinet and find a steady leak. God damn it. I just had this thing replaced.

"Willow. Kitchen floors aren't made for swimming."

"But we had fun!"

"Is Daisy wet?"

The dog in question comes running into the kitchen. My golden retriever is anything but golden.

"Willow." I take a deep inhale in, trying to infuse every part of me with patience this morning.

This is not how I wanted to start my day.

"Yeah, Daddy?"

"Why is Daisy blue?"

"Because my hands were wet and I had to wipe them off when I was done painting." Willow looks so innocent, like this isn't a big deal at all.

"Then why is your dress blue?"

"Because I gave Daisy a hug."

Deep breath, Mason. She's seven.

Finding the water valve, I shut it off, watching the water slow before coming to a stop. It's going to cost me a pretty penny to get someone out here to fix it today.

"Okay. Willow, how wet is your dress?"

"Not that wet." I know she's saying that so she can keep wearing it.

"Why don't we go give Daisy a bath and then get you into some dry clothes."

Willow pops her bottom lip out at me in a frown. I know I won't like what she has to say next. And it usually means I'll cave.

"But I wanted to wear my princess outfit today."

"Don't you have another one?"

"You washed it yesterday because I played outside in it and got it muddy."

"Right." Picking her up so she doesn't get more water everywhere, I carry her into the laundry room.

The ranch house I bought a few years ago is small, but it's the perfect size for the two of us. Willow has her own space on one side of the house, and I have my room on the other. The living room isn't huge, but I don't care. Neither does Willow. It's so packed full of pink and glitter that I'm glad it's condensed to a smaller space.

If it were any bigger, it'd explode with Willow's personality.

Girl is all about glitter and painting anything she can find right now.

"Damn it."

The laundry I did yesterday is still sitting in the washing machine.

"Does that mean I can't wear it?" Willow asks, peeping over my shoulder.

"No." I set her down on top of the dryer while I start the load again. "Why don't you wear that new hoodie Uncle Logan got you?"

Willow crosses her arms in a pout. "But I wanted to wear my dress!"

I pinch the space between my eyebrows. Coffee is needed before I can deal with a little girl who can't wear what she wants to. "Pipsqueak, I'm sorry. But you know, if you wear the sweatshirt today, you can wear the dress tomorrow."

"Will it be clean?"

If I remember to put it in the dryer when I get home. "Yes. I promise you it'll be clean."

"Okay. I'll wear my sweatshirt."

She hops off the machine and runs through the kitchen.

"Not through the water!"

I hear her giggles as she splashes through.

Is it too early to go back to bed and start this day over?

Being a single dad is one of the best and hardest things I've ever done. With Willow's mom stationed overseas and agreeing that Willow should stay in Dixon to not uproot her entire life, all responsibility falls to me.

Not that I mind. I love every minute I get to spend with that little girl. But mornings like this one make me wish I had an extra set of hands. Someone to remember the laundry. Someone to make the coffee.

Hell, someone to just get up with her so I can get more than four hours of sleep after working all night.

It's not going to do me any good right now. Starting the washer, I shut the lid and grab old towels to start mopping up the water.

The coffee machine finally kicks on—thank God that's automatic—and I head back to Willow's room. She's sitting on the floor reading Daisy a book. Daisy's muzzle is resting in her lap as Willow strokes the not-entirely-yellow fur on her head.

"And they lived happily ever after." Willow drops a kiss on Daisy's head. "That's my favorite part."

"Okay, Willow. Let's get Daisy cleaned up, and then we can get breakfast at the diner before we go and see Uncle Peter."

Willow sighs. "Does that mean you're working today?"

I nod. "I know, I'm sorry. But Uncle Peter needs my help." And the last thing I want to do is let down another one of my siblings. "I promise we won't be long, and you can get pancakes for breakfast."

Her tiny face screws up in thought, considering my answer. "Can I get chocolate chips on my pancakes?"

"As long as we have fruit with it too."

Willow would eat nothing but sweets if I let her.

"None of the mushy orange stuff though. I don't like that."

"Gross. No one likes cantaloupe."

"But yes to chocolate chips."

"Let's get Daisy cleaned up first. I don't want her staying blue forever."

Willow giggles. "She'd look funny blue."

"She does. Next time get a paper towel instead of using her, okay?"

"Okay, Daddy."

Willow helps get Daisy into the bath. My four-legged kid is well trained, getting lathered up and rinsed off without a whine.

"I don't think the paint is coming off," Willow says, pouring another cup of water over Daisy's fur.

Green. She's tinted green. My poor girl who loves Willow more than she loves me looks like she's getting moldy.

"Are we going to have to cut her fur off?" Willow asks, looking like she wants to cry. "I didn't mean to turn her green."

"I know. We'll give her another bath tomorrow and she should be fine."

Drying her off, Willow gives her a kiss before going to get changed.

"You're my good girl, aren't you?" Her tongue hangs out of her mouth. "Hopefully you won't stay green forever."

The rest of the day goes by without incident. Even though I'm dragging Willow all over town to help my brother, she keeps herself busy with coloring books and reading to Daisy.

I wish it wasn't like this. I hate that she can't be outside running around on an early spring day like this one. With my family all just as busy, there's no one that I can readily rely on to watch her.

By the time we get home, I'm exhausted. Every muscle in my body aches like I just ran a marathon and not worked my regular Saturday. If possible, today was even longer than yesterday. There aren't enough hours in the day for me to get everything I need done. With things getting busier at the bar, it's going to mean a lot more days like today, working myself to the bone with not enough time spent with my daughter.

Who is now curling up in my lap, ready to read a book before bed.

"Daddy. Is my dress clean?"

Damn it.

Fucking laundry.

Canon
EOS
600D
M LENS EF-S 18-55mm 1:3.5-5.6 IS

Chapter Two

IVY

I hate this town.

After picking up my coffee—at the only coffee shop in town—before my hike, I was stopped no less than three times by the town's historical romance book club. All the older women in town belong. Since I got home from school in January, they've been asking me about my love life.

Okay, maybe hate is a strong word.

But why is the only way I can be successful is if I settle down?

I'm in a huffy mood by the time I meet Gemma at the trailhead.

Her brown hair is tucked away under a winter hat. Winter still has its stranglehold on the weather. Spring is trying to arrive, but nothing.

"What's got you in a mood?"

I zip up my black down jacket, burrowing farther into it. "Mrs. Reynolds."

Gemma nods. "Say no more. What was it today?"

"How in the Victorian times I would be considered an old hag because I'm not married."

"Seriously?"

I nod. "You're lucky you get your coffee from the ranch."

"What can I say?" She gives me her brightest smile. "One of the perks of living and working there."

"Ready to get going?" I loop my arm through hers and take off on the easy walking trail between the town's main drag and the mountains beyond.

"I feel like I haven't seen you in months," Gemma tells me.

"I saw you two weeks ago."

"So sue me. It feels like longer. It's been so busy with ski season ending at the ranch."

"I'll miss it next year."

The ground is hard beneath our feet. With the temps dropping last night, a frost descended on the town.

"You know you can always come visit. Seattle isn't that far."

I snort laugh, my breath coming out in puffs around me. "It's a twelve-hour drive, Gem. I'll be a lowly art intern. I won't be able to afford coming back."

"You're right. You should just stay in Dixon."

"As if that's a likely possibility."

The crisp mountain air is cold as I suck in a deep breath. Early spring is my favorite time in Dixon. The trails are empty of people.

"Have you found a place yet?"

I shake my head. "Not yet. I want to be downtown, but I can't afford anything in that area."

"I can always come out and help you look. I've always wanted to go to Seattle."

We veer with the trail. The trees are barren. I stop Gemma and take out my camera to snap a picture.

"I know. But I want to do it on my own."

Gemma rolls her eyes at me as she sips her coffee. "You don't always have to."

"If my mother gets wind of you helping, she'll think I didn't tell her because I wanted to have my dad come help instead."

"Still?"

I nod, shoving my phone back into my pocket, happy with how the picture turned out. "You know her."

My parents have been divorced—and unhappy with each other—for as long as I can remember. When I was a kid, I thought things would get better after they left each other. Didn't do me any good. They just used me against each other.

I hated it. It's one of the many reasons I want to get out of this town.

Not that either of them live here anymore. Mom left as soon as I turned eighteen. Dad at least waited until I graduated to move down south. He's a bit more tolerable now that he got remarried.

Mom? She's still a pain.

And this town doesn't hold the best of memories for me. It's the reason I want to leave so badly.

"We just have to keep it quiet. I don't want you having to move there all by yourself."

I laugh, turning up the trail again. Cold starts to burn my lungs. I love the feeling, exerting myself like this.

"Gem, I will be okay. I'm a big girl. I can live in a city by myself."

She stops, pulling me to a stop with her. The sun is starting to slip behind the clouds, taking its heat with it.

"It'll make me feel better about you leaving. I want to make sure you're safe wherever you land there."

I pull Gemma into a hug. She is the one person I'm going to miss in town. Whenever I didn't want to be at my house when I was little, I was always welcome at the Winchesters'. With five kids, I was never made to feel like I was bothering anyone.

"Fine. You can come. But you're buying breakfast this morning. I bought last week."

"Deal." Linking arms again, we head back down. "Now let's go, because I'm starving."

"YOU COULD ALWAYS HAVE a fun summer fling before you leave," Gemma says, grabbing a menu as we sit at one of the only free tables at the diner.

It's everything a small-town diner should be. Vintage ads hang on the walls. Black-and-white checkered floors are dull after being worn down for years. Vinyl seats crack as people sit in any open seats they can find. People linger at the counter seats where they can watch food being made in the kitchen.

"I'm sorry, you're telling me this? Miss 'I hate every single man in Dixon.'"

"I have good reason to."

"Oh, I know. Which is shocking you're telling me to have a summer fling."

"I'm just saying, it could be a fun thing for you to do." Gemma shrugs a shoulder. I know she means well, but it's not really on my mind right now.

The waitress comes by and takes our order. The place is bustling. It's one of the only places to be on a weekend morning.

"You know the people in this town. There are no good options."

"What about in Jackson?"

"Gemma, I love you for trying, but no. I'll be content on my own this summer. Seattle won't know what hit them when I get there."

"Gemma. Ivy. How are you girls doing?" Mrs. Phillips, head of the town gossip committee, comes over to our table.

"Hi, Mrs. Phillips. We're good," I answer for us. "How are you doing?"

"Wonderful. What brings you two out on a fine morning like this?" She slides into the empty seat on Gemma's side of the booth.

Gemma eyes me. "We were just talking about Ivy's new job in Seattle."

"Seattle?" Her eyes go wide, her graying hair perfect. Not a hair out of place. "How can you even think of moving away from Dixon?"

I paste a fake smile on my face. First the book club this morning, and now Mrs. Phillips. I need to keep it together. I like the women in this town, but sometimes they drive me crazy.

"You know I want to run an art gallery."

She waves me off. "Why do you need to buy art from a gallery? If I want something, I can just go online and get it."

And now she sounds like my mother. If possible, the smile on my face grows. The bigger it is, the less chance I'll let something slip. "Some people still like buying it in person. You get a better feel for the piece when you see it."

"Are you sure you don't want us to set you up with a nice man? Settle down in Dixon? Seattle is such a violent city." She shudders.

"I'll be safe. Don't you worry."

She gasps, clasping her hands over her heart. "Of

course we'll worry. You couldn't have tried Boise? Now that's a perfectly fine town."

"Seattle has more to offer me in the art world."

She ignores me, turning to Gemma.

"Aren't your brothers single, Gemma?" She slaps her hand on the table like she's had the most genius idea. I know exactly where she's going, and I don't think I'll like it. "Why can't you set her up with one of them?"

Yup. Exactly where I thought.

"What?" Gemma looks affronted. "My brothers?"

"Of course. They're all so handsome."

Based on the side-eye Mrs. Phillips gives me, I do a bad job suppressing my laugh. I know Gemma is squirming inside at her comments.

"Peter is taken. Logan isn't thinking about dating, and Mason has Willow."

"What a shame. All those good genes going to waste." She stands, clapping Gemma on the shoulder. "I'll let you girls get back to it."

"Bye!" We both wave her off.

"Can you imagine you with one of my brothers?" Gemma grabs the mimosa that is set in front of her. I take my own gulp, trying to push down all the thoughts that Mrs. Phillips brought up.

"I can't even. It's laughable," I tell Gemma.

But it's not.

Because for as long as I've known Gemma, I've known her entire family.

Including her oldest brother, Mason.

There's something about him. I don't know if it's because he's so much older, but his chiseled features have always drawn my eyes.

Hard muscles. Long brown hair on top, but shaved on the sides.

I notice everything about him.

I've had a crush on Mason Winchester since I knew what those feelings meant. But because of the woman across from me, I never acted on them. She's my family.

And I would never do anything to jeopardize that.

No matter how much I want to experience what it'd be like to kiss him.

Just once.

Chapter Three

MASON

"I don't think we should do it."

"I'm sorry, what?"

I couldn't have heard Peter correctly.

"I think we should push back canning The Clara."

There's a really bad joke in there, but right now, I'm a little too pissed at my brother potentially dropping a huge opportunity.

"Why?"

Peter scrubs a hand down his face, looking more tired than he has in the last few weeks combined. "It's just not the right time. With everything going on with Logan, we don't need to be taking on more work here."

"Weren't you just telling me how stagnant everything has become?"

Peter throws the papers on the ever growing pile that's on his desk. "Stagnant isn't bad. We're fine for now. Why rock the boat?"

Nash comes into the office.

"Will you reason with him?"

"On what?"

"He doesn't want to start canning The Clara."

"He wants to can it?" Nash looks delighted with himself.

"Walked into that one." I laugh.

"You know how busy things are at home," Peter protests.

I try to cut him off, but he doesn't let me.

"And don't say you can help out more with Logan. You're already overworking yourself as it is."

Nothing like your little brother chastising you for working too much.

Instead, I go in for the kill shot. "You know Logan wouldn't want you putting this off because of him."

Peter narrows his eyes at me. "You're a bastard, you know that?"

I give him my best smile. "Don't I know it."

Nash walks over to Peter, sitting on his desk. "Peter. It's a good idea. I know you're scared, but that's why you have me and Mason."

Peter blows out a breath. "Mason, can you give Nash and me a minute?"

Having walked in on them one too many times fooling around in his office, I bolt out of there. That's the last thing I want to see burned into my memory for all of time.

Only to find Ivy Connors—Gemma's best friend— tapping her fingers against the bar top.

She doesn't notice me, but I sure as fuck notice her.

The way her long brown hair falls over one shoulder. The glint of the nose piercing she has. The way her lips look pillow soft and curve into a small smile when she sees me.

I should not be noticing my little sister's best friend.

"Ivy." I grab the counter, willing it to hold me back from noticing anything more about this tempting woman.

"Hey. Can I get The Clara please?"

"Sure thing."

The routine of mixing the bar's most popular cocktail —potato vodka and ginger beer with a splash of grenadine —helps to calm my racing thoughts.

I never turn into someone who can't keep his cool around women. Not that I'm some womanizing dick, but I've never had a problem before.

"Here you go."

"Thanks."

Her fingers brush over mine as she grabs the drink. It sends heat pooling in my groin.

What in the actual fuck? That's never happened before.

Ivy's eyes don't meet my own as I hand over the drink.

There's no way she could have felt something, could she?

My phone buzzes in my pocket. Normally, I wouldn't answer it, but seeing as how it's slow for a Saturday afternoon, I know it's fine.

I could also use the distraction from Ivy.

"Gramps. Hey."

"Hey Mason. Everything is okay, but Willow says her throat hurts," Gramps tells me.

Damn it. This has been happening more and more. After our last visit to the doctor this past winter, he said if they don't get better, she'd have to get her tonsils taken out this summer.

"Can you give—"

"Already given her something to help. She's eating a popsicle now with Daisy."

I blow out a breath. "Thanks, Gramps. I owe you."

"No, you don't. It's what family does."

"I hate that I'm not there for her." As I'm convincing

my brother to make my life even crazier by taking on this new venture.

"She's fine. I'm going to put on a movie for her, and she can fall asleep to it if she wants."

"Tell her I'll be there to pick her up soon." Even though the bar is starting to fill up, I can call someone in to help. One of the perks of managing the front of house staff.

"Don't rush." Gramps chuckles before hanging up on me.

"Everything okay?" Ivy asks, sipping on her drink. The look on her face tells me she heard every minute of that conversation.

"Willow isn't feeling too good."

"Anything I can do to help?"

"Add like six more pairs of hands and eighteen more hours to the day and I'm set."

"Well, I can't do that, but Gemma mentioned you might need some help with Willow."

"She did?" Damn it. I told her I had it covered. No one in my family can keep their mouth shut.

Willow's mom is in the army and is stationed overseas. She loves it, and I can't fault her for her dedication to her country.

We were friends in high school, and after dating for a few months one summer and calling it quits, she ended up pregnant. We decided we were better as friends, and we share custody of Willow but agreed when she got this overseas assignment that it would be best for Willow to stay with me. And while our situation usually works, I'm spread thinner and thinner these days.

"I'm not really doing much before I leave, so if you need help…"

"I don't."

Ivy rolls her eyes. "So you're not burning the candle at both ends?"

"He is," Nash pipes up as he grabs a bottle of vodka behind me.

"Fucker," I mumble under my breath.

"I'm actually pretty good with kids if you want me to help out with Willow."

"I can't ask you to do that."

"You're not asking me to." Ivy sets down her now empty drink.

"You want another?"

She shakes her head. "No. I'm off to go take some pictures. Gemma said you were being stubborn, so I figured I'd stop by and chat."

"Next time you see my sister, tell her to mind her own business."

I love her, but damn, she keeps trying to nose her way into my business.

"Nash talked me back into it," Peter says, walking by me to help a customer that sat down at the other end of the bar. He looks all too happy right now.

"I really don't want to know details," I groan.

"What's that all about?" Ivy sets a twenty down on the bar for me.

"You don't want to know."

She nods in understanding. "You know where to find me if you need help."

I should let her go. Walk off and not draw her into my world. Gemma already gave me her number.

My brain is at war—wanting to call her back but pushing her away.

But I need the help. More than I care to admit. I can bury these weird feelings she stirs up inside of me and let her help.

Calling her feels like I'm failing at the one job in the world I can't fail at.

"Ivy," I call out after her retreating form.

"Yeah?"

"Can you come over tomorrow morning? I know it's a Sunday, but—"

"I'll be there."

Let's just hope I don't regret this decision.

Chapter Four

MASON

"Will Ivy play with me and Daisy?" Willow tosses another treat to the dog in question.

"I don't know why she wouldn't."

"Daisy will be sad if no one plays with her."

Our dog's tongue is hanging out of her mouth, and she's as happy as a clam. Anytime she's with Willow, she's happy.

"Willow, honey, Daisy will be fine. I want to make sure you like Ivy."

"But I already know Ivy." The duh in her tone is implied. Lord help me when this girl gets to the teenage years. "If Daisy doesn't like her, I won't like her."

"When has Daisy not liked anyone? She even likes our mail lady."

Willow giggles. "That's because she gives her treats."

"Do I need to tell Ivy that she needs to give Daisy treats? Will that help?" Daisy barks at me as the doorbell rings.

"She's here!" Willow shouts before grabbing Daisy's

head and focusing on her. "Make sure to give Ivy lots of kisses. I want her to be my nanny."

Dropping a kiss on her furry head, Willow runs to my side.

"Do you think she'll like me too?"

I drop down to her level, ignoring the fact that I'm keeping Ivy waiting.

Everything about me has been fighting this for weeks. I need help with my daughter. My brother needs help at the bar, and I don't want to let another sibling down.

"Of course she's going to like you. Everyone does, Pipsqueak."

She nods, firming up her face.

Finally, I open the door, and Ivy Connors is waiting on the other side.

Gemma's best friend.

The woman that has driven me crazy every time I've seen her since her twenty-first birthday.

My eyes take too long of a perusal. Oversized sweater that hangs off one shoulder. Tight leggings that show off her long legs. Light-brown hair that falls down her body in perfect waves.

And why is that gold nose ring of hers so fucking hot?

"Hey Willow!" She addresses my daughter first, breaking me out of my obvious staring.

"Do you like dogs?" Willow asks.

"Of course I like dogs. Where is Daisy?"

Willow's eyes go wide. "You know Daisy?"

"What a silly question. She's been out at the ranch."

"You need to come see her again." Willow grabs Ivy's hand and pulls her into the house, completely forgetting about me.

"Hey, Mason." Ivy gives me a smile as she brushes by me.

Why does she smell so damn good? A little woodsy, a little floral.

Ivy is down on the living room floor with Willow and Daisy, chattering away with them. I should've known it would be this easy.

Willow loves everyone. Of course she's going to love Ivy too. She's Gemma's best friend.

It's what makes her being Willow's nanny so dangerous.

I've always felt this pull to Ivy. But something in these last few years has made it grow. I've tried to keep my distance from her. Distance keeps me safe.

But with her now being in my house, potentially every fucking day, I'm going to lose my mind.

How could I *not* with having this captivating woman in my space.

"What do you like to do after school?" Ivy asks Willow.

"I read books. And color. And play with Daisy. And sometimes Daddy takes me hiking."

Ivy's gaze flits to mine before going back to Willow's. "I'm really good at coloring."

"Is that what you do after school?" Willow asks.

Ivy laughs. "Well, I'm not in school anymore."

Those words remind me just how young she is. She's Gemma's age, for Christ's sake. Ten years younger than I am.

I do not need to be lusting after someone so much younger.

"So what do you do?" Willow asks.

"I like taking pictures."

"Of people?"

"People. Mountains. Anything really."

"That's cool. Maybe you could take a picture of Daisy."

Ivy pets Daisy's head, which is now resting on her lap. Even my damn dog is smitten with her. "We'll have to do that."

I haven't even hired her yet, and they're acting like this is a done deal. I need to slow this train down before it gets out of control.

"Willow, go out back and play, will ya?"

"Okay, Daddy." She hops up and runs out the back. "See you tomorrow, Ivy!"

"You know, you shouldn't lead her on like that."

"How am I leading her on?" Ivy stands up, brushing off the backs of her legs.

"Telling her you'll take pictures of Daisy. I don't want her getting her hopes up."

"Do you have a problem with me?" Ivy crosses her arms, turning those big blue eyes on me.

Fuck. Why am I so taken with this woman?

"Why do you think I have a problem with you?"

She waves her hand in front of me. "Because everything about you says you do."

"No, it doesn't." I drop my crossed arms.

"Look, do you need my help or not?"

I scrub a hand down my face. "I do, and I don't want to leave Willow with just anyone. It's harder with her mom gone and not having any help."

"Then let me help you. Mason, you've known me my entire life."

"So you know that little girl is my whole world."

"I know that. So you can trust me with her. She will be well taken care of." A smile plays on her lips. I like it. Maybe a little too much. "Besides, there's no shortage of Winchesters in this town if I ever needed anything."

I blow out the breath I've been holding, trying to release the tension in my shoulders.

Ivy is the answer to all my problems. Willow likes her. Daisy likes her. Hell, I even like her. Probably too much for my sanity.

But something's gotta give. Otherwise I'm going to crack under all the pressure I'm putting on myself.

"I'll need help after school for a few hours. Dinner. Maybe some bedtimes. Then once school lets out, every day during the week. And spring break is this week, so she's off school. Maybe the occasional Saturday if Peter needs me at the bar."

Ivy gives me a once-over. It unsettles me how she's watching me. It shouldn't, considering I was just doing the same thing to her. "Gemma told you I'm leaving at the end of August, right?"

"She did. Once we start canning, everything should slow down, and I can be there for Willow after school."

"Canning?" Ivy screws up a brow. "What are you guys canning?"

"The Clara."

"Holy shit, Mason. That's really cool."

I rest my elbows on the counter, leaning in closer to her. From here, I can see light flecks of gold in her eyes.

"I'm really hoping it works. I pushed Peter into doing it, and I'd hate for him to have to fire his older brother."

"Why wouldn't it work?" Ivy settles onto the barstool.

I shrug a shoulder. "Just like with any new venture, it could completely flop."

"Not that my opinion means much, but I love The Clara."

"You have to say that."

"No I don't. Trust me, if it wasn't any good, I wouldn't get it every time I go to The Tipsy Cocktail. I think it's a good idea."

"You do?" Why am I seeking confirmation from Ivy on

this? It's not like I need her to validate how I'm feeling about this.

"I think it'll be great for the bar. Especially with this big music fest you're planning this summer."

"Not me, thank God. There aren't enough hours in the day for me to do that. But that's what I've been trying to tell Peter this whole time. He's so wrapped up with Nash and Logan that it's hard for him to see that it can be a really good thing."

"And I'll be here to help you if you need me." I can hear the question in her tone. Anyone who wants to hang out with my crazy kid is good in my book.

I'll just have to push my feelings for her down and bury them.

Willow chooses that moment to come running into the house with Daisy, yelling and giggling as mud sticks to the floor behind them as they race to her room.

One more thing to add to my ever growing to-do list.

Ivy is fighting a smile.

"Are you sure you know what you're signing on for?" I quirk a brow at her.

"If that's the worst of it, I think so."

At least I can cross something off that list.

"Can you start tomorrow?"

Canon
M LENS EF-S 18-55mm 1:3.5-5.6
EOS
600D

Chapter Five

IVY

"Are you nervous for your first day?" Gemma's voice is loud through the car speakers.

"No. I like Willow. We had a good time together yesterday."

I don't tell her that the part I'm nervous about is Mason. He was fine the day I came over.

That's it.

Just fine.

Maybe if he acts indifferent to me like he did that day, I'll be okay. It'll crush these simmering feelings I've always had for him.

"Well, if you need anything, let me know. I can pop over real fast."

I turn onto their street. "I'll be fine, Ivy. How bad could it be? She's seven."

Gemma laughs at me. "Good luck, Ive. Call me when you leave."

"Bye, babe."

I hang up and park the car outside the small ranch home. Sidewalk chalk covers the driveway. Two stick figures are holding hands with what looks to be a dog next to them. I can only smile. The telltale signs of Willow.

Knocking on the door, noise hits my ears.

"Hi, Ivy!" Willow opens the door, covered in glitter.

"Hi, Willow." A bark comes from the back of the house as the smoke alarm starts to beep. "Is everything okay?"

She nods, shutting the door behind me. I drop my bag down next to the entry table as Daisy rounds the corner. Her tail is wagging, covered in ribbons.

"Doesn't Daisy look pretty? She wanted to play dress-up with me."

"Daisy looks pretty, but not as pretty as you."

Willow beams up at me. She crooks her finger down and I bend to meet her height. "Daddy burned my pancakes."

That much is obvious.

"Why don't we go help him?"

Willow grabs my hand and drags me through to the kitchen. It's a newer house, but you couldn't tell with all the drawings tacked up. Everything from rainbows and unicorns to pictures of Daisy line most of the space. You can hardly see the gray walls through it all.

"Ivy's here, Daddy."

Mason's hard gaze meets mine. It sends a tingle down my spine.

Why is it so hot when he stares at me like that?

"You're early."

I tap my phone. "I'm two minutes early, Mason."

"Fuck." He checks his own watch and blows out a breath. "I'm running late. And I burned breakfast."

Willow giggles from her perch on the barstool.

"Why don't I get this cleaned up and you can head out."

"I didn't mean to leave you with this mess." Mason looks sympathetic as he turns those brown eyes on me.

"I can handle it." He looks like he's going to fight me on it, but drops the burnt pan in the sink.

"Daisy's already been fed. She could probably use a walk,"—he drops his voice to whisper the last word—"and I should probably be home by five or six. I'll take care of dinner."

"Can we get takeout so you don't burn it?" Willow asks.

"Damn. Tough critic."

"You burned my grilled cheese last week."

"Hey! I did not. It never cooked enough to burn," Mason defends.

I pat Mason on the arm. "I don't think that's the defense you think it is."

"It was yucky." Willow screws up her face in disgust.

"Maybe I can make you a grilled cheese for lunch and then you can show your dad how to do it."

"Okay. I never get to help cook."

I throw a wink in Willow's direction. "I'll teach you lots of new things."

"This is going to be so fun."

Mason steps around me, dropping a kiss on Willow's head. "Be good, Willow. Make sure to listen to what Ivy says and don't talk back."

"I never talk back."

"Then I know you'll be a good girl for Ivy. And make sure to pick up your toys when you're done playing."

Willow gives him a kiss on the cheek. "Okay. I love you, Daddy."

"Love you too, Pipsqueak. And remember what I said about painting?"

She hangs her head, looking sad for the first time. "No painting unless Daddy is here to supervise."

Mason waves goodbye as he heads out the door.

"Looks like it's just us girls." Willow is staring up at me with wide, brown eyes. Eyes that look exactly like her dad's.

Now that Mason is gone, the nerves have settled in. Not that I'm worried about taking care of her, but I want her to have fun. I know what it was like to be an only child. Except her childhood is already so much different from mine.

"Am I going to have to eat cereal for breakfast? I really wanted pancakes."

Leaning on the counter, I get on Willow's level. "Do you have another pan? I can make you my special pancakes."

"Your special pancakes?" Willow hops out of the chair and runs around the counter, digging in a cabinet. Her tiny arms heft out another pan, just like the one sitting in the sink. "Gramps got Daddy another pan because he said he doesn't know how to cook."

"I guess that means we're making pancakes!"

"Can you show me how to make them?"

"Sure." Turning on the sink, I soak the pan that is covered in burned pancake batter.

Poor Mason. Maybe if he wasn't running late, he wouldn't have burned them. Based on today alone, he's running himself ragged.

Hopefully by the end of today, he'll stop worrying about leaving Willow with me and he'll relax a bit.

"Okay. Grab the bananas. We're going to add them to the mix."

"Bananas? I've never had bananas in pancakes before."

"You haven't? They are my favorite."

"How do we make them?"

Grabbing the still half-full bowl of batter, I dig around in the drawers to find another spatula. "You get the fun part and are going to smash the banana."

"Daddy never lets me do that."

"Well, today you can. Where are the plates?"

Willow points to a cabinet behind my head. Grabbing one, I hand it to her with a fork and peel the banana.

"Now you smush it."

"Like this?" She smashes the fork into the banana, watching it squish out on all sides.

"Yes. Do that to the whole thing and then we'll mix it in with the batter."

Willow is giddy as she finishes the simple job I gave her.

It's something I never got to do growing up. I taught myself to cook in college. It was either that or live off takeout.

"That's great, Willow. Now, mix it into the batter and then I'll show you how to cook them."

Willow does exactly as I ask, her face a mask of concentration. It's quite possibly the cutest thing ever.

"That looks good. Now, when it starts to bubble,"—I pour a scoop of the batter onto the now sizzling pan— "we'll flip it."

"I don't think Daddy knows how to do that."

"Maybe he just forgot. He's really busy."

"I can show him how to do it."

Willow isn't looking at me though. She's studying the pan. As soon as the first few bubbles break the surface, her eyes are wide.

"Look, Ivy!"

"Let's let a few more bubble up and then we'll flip it."

"This is so fun."

It shouldn't take the excitement of a seven-year-old to make me happy, but it does. Her excitement is contagious.

"Is it ready to flip now?"

"Yes." Grabbing the spatula, I steady it and then give it a quick flip. It's the perfect golden color.

"That looks a lot better than Daddy's."

"You can be his sous chef."

"What's that?"

"Assistant chef."

Willow nods, watching the rest of the pancake cook.

"It's ready." Scooping it off the pan, I drop it onto the plate that was already sitting on the counter.

"Give it a minute. It's still hot."

"Can I blow on it?"

"Sure."

I smile at her. This girl is so full of life. She loves asking questions and wants to do things. Even if it's as simple as making her breakfast.

I cut it up into smaller bites for her and push it in her direction. "Okay. Now you can try. Tell me what you think."

"Delicious!" Her cheeks are stuffed full.

"Thanks for your help."

"Can we make them tomorrow?"

I take my own bite. Damn. These really are good. "Maybe. Or maybe I'll teach you to make something else."

The rest of the day is spent doing anything Willow wants.

Reading. Playing outside. Convincing her that coloring is better than painting. Before I know it, most of the day has passed.

"Why don't we take Daisy for a walk? I think your dad will be home soon."

"Okay. Daisy!" Willow shouts for her, but she's only snoozing on the couch. "It's walk time."

Daisy is beside herself with excitement as she leaps off the couch. Willow gets her leash and clips it on. Clearly this is a routine that they do all the time.

"Make sure you hold my hand, okay?"

"I know." Willow rolls her eyes at me. "Daddy tells me I have to stay on the inside of the sidewalk."

"Okay. Get your coat then."

Willow slips into her hot-pink coat and we're out the door. A breeze has picked up, bringing a chill with it. Linking my hand with Willow's, Daisy steers us down the sidewalk. For being so excited, she's good on her leash.

"Are you coming back tomorrow?" Willow asks.

"Of course I am."

"Are we going to do more fun things? I like not being in school."

"You don't like school?"

"I do, but I like playing at home. I think Daisy gets sad when I'm not home. Daddy too."

"Your dad has fun going to work. He likes seeing Peter and Nash."

"I wish I had a brother or sister to play with."

"I didn't have a brother or sister growing up."

"You didn't?"

"Just me. But you're lucky and have a lot of friends to play with you."

"I do have a lot of friends." Willow goes into a long-winded explanation of all her friends at school, and why some are meany-heads—her words—and who the best freeze tag people are.

Crossing the street at the end of the road, the neighborhood opens up to a wide field that stretches all the way to the Tetons in the distance.

It's beautiful.

"Look!" I point to the field of dandelions. The fuzzy white blooms are blowing in the wind, spreading their seeds everywhere. "Have you ever made a wish on dandelions?"

Willow shakes her head.

"Here." I hand her the fluffiest one I can find. Daisy is dutifully sitting next to her, watching her. "Now, make a wish inside your head and blow."

Closing her eyes, Willow takes a deep breath and blows.

"Hurry! Open them!"

She watches as all the seeds get carried off into the wind. "It's taking my wish!"

"Maybe it'll come true."

"I didn't know you could make a wish on those." Willow picks another. "Can I make more wishes?"

I shake my head. "If you want your first wish to come true, you don't want to make too many."

"Can we take them home then? I can give them to Daddy to make a wish."

"That is a great idea, Willow."

This little girl has the biggest heart. I hold on to Daisy's leash as she grabs a few more yellow ones to add to her growing bundle.

"There. Daddy will like these."

"He'll like them because you picked them."

By the time we get home, Mason's truck is in the drive-way. Nerves gather in my belly. I know we had a fun day, but I don't want to disappoint Mason.

"Daddy!" Willow takes off, running to him.

I know how much he loves this little girl, and I wanted her to have the best day too.

"You're home earlier than I thought." Mason is sitting on the porch.

He gives me a warm smile. This time, it's butterflies exploding in my stomach.

Damn it. I shouldn't be having these kinds of feelings for Mason.

"I'm sure you'd be surprised by this,"—Mason pushes up to stand, his muscles flexing—"but when your attention isn't pulled in a million directions, work is much more efficient."

"Glad I could help."

"Did you have a fun day?" Mason turns his attention to Willow.

Willow leaps into Mason's arms. I'm exhausted. We've been going all day, and she is still full of energy. I don't know how she does it.

"Ivy is so cool! She showed me how to make pancakes and we made wishes on dandelions on our walk with Daisy!" She thrusts the tiny bundle of weeds in his face. "These are for you!"

"I love them."

"I can't wait for Ivy to come back tomorrow."

"Me too." Mason is looking me dead in the eyes. "We'll see you tomorrow?" Mason asks.

Does he know he's driving me crazy? The way he is with his daughter is tugging at my heartstrings.

I didn't think that this crush would get any worse when I took this job, but I guess I was wrong. Seeing this grumpy guy, who doesn't want help and wants to do everything on his own, holding this precious little girl, is enough to melt even the iciest of hearts.

"Yeah, see you tomorrow."

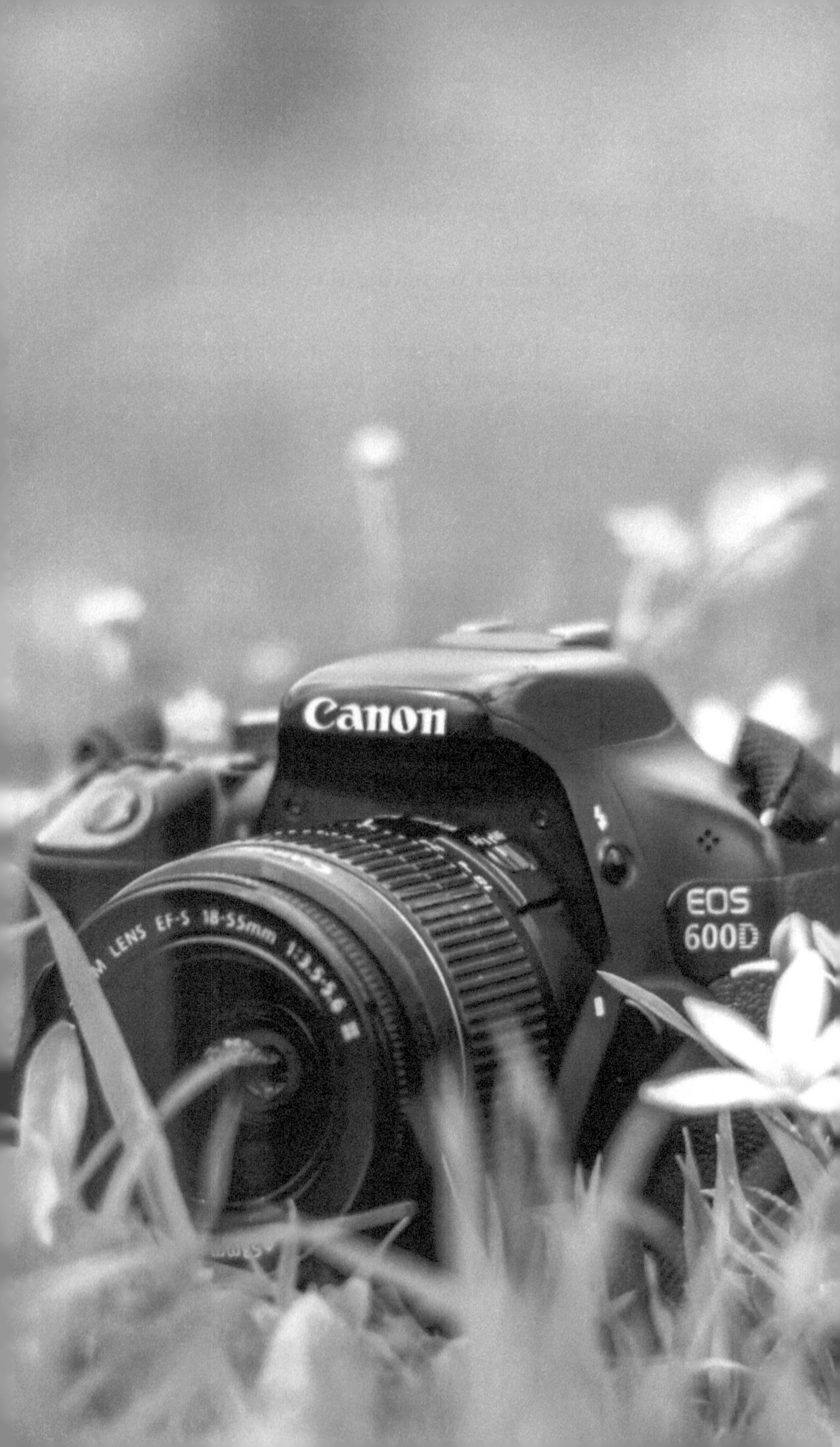
Canon
EOS
600D
LENS EF-S 18-55mm 1:3.5-5.6

Chapter Six

IVY

"Thanks for coming on a Saturday," Mason tells me again. He's been apologetic ever since calling me over here this morning.

"It's fine. Really."

"Logan just needs some help with a few things, and I should be back by one."

"Really, it's not a big deal." I grab his forearm, squeezing it. Heat shoots through my arm.

Damn it. I really hate the reaction I keep having to Mason. I don't want it. I'm only going to be in town for a short while longer. Starting something now would be stupid.

Even though I'd love every minute of it.

"She should be awake soon."

"Get going. We'll be fine."

I drop his arm, feeling the loss of heat in an instant.

Gemma's older brother. Gemma's older brother.

Maybe if I keep telling myself that, it'll help.

Giving me a small smile—very un-Mason-like—he's out the door.

It's almost like he couldn't get out of here fast enough.

His scent lingers as I grab a cup of coffee.

God, I really wish this man didn't occupy every one of my waking thoughts. It was fine when I didn't work for him. Now? Now I have to figure out how to deal with these feelings. Feelings that I've had since I knew what crushes were.

Footsteps from the hallway help shake the thoughts of Mason from my head. Even if it's his mini-me coming around the corner.

"Ivy? What are you doing here?" She rubs a fist over a sleepy eye. Her curls are sticking out every which way.

"Your dad had to go help Uncle Logan today."

"He did?" Her voice sounds sad.

"It's okay though. You get to hang out with me this morning!" I try to add some excitement to my voice.

"Daddy and I had a fun day planned." Willow hops up onto the stool at the counter.

"What were you going to do?" I grab the box of cereal and milk and pour it into a bowl for her.

"He was going to take me hiking."

"Do you and your daddy go hiking a lot?"

She nods around a big bite of chocolatey cereal.

"I can take you if you want."

"You like hiking?" Willow turns those big brown eyes on me.

"Of course I do. Who doesn't like hiking?"

"Mark doesn't. He stays inside and plays video games all day."

"Mark…someone from school?"

Willow nods.

"Well, who cares what he thinks?" I rest my elbows on the counter and lean closer to her. "Boys can be stupid."

"Boys are stupid." Willow says it with such fervor, it makes me burst into a fit of giggles.

"They really are. But we don't need them today."

"No." Willow shoves the last bite of cereal in her mouth. "You'll really take me?"

"Of course I will. It can be our very own special day together."

Her eyes light up. "Just like I have with Daddy!"

"Exactly. Now go get dressed."

Willow gives me a hug before rushing off.

It's something that I never got to do when I was her age. At that point, my parents were at each other's throats, so I escaped to Gemma's most days.

At least with Willow's mom gone, I can hopefully give her some special days, even if Mason isn't around for them.

Grabbing my phone, I shoot a text off to Mason.

> Taking Willow hiking...be back later this afternoon

IT TAKES him a minute to respond.

MASON

> Thx

JUST LIKE MASON. One-word answer. I shouldn't let it bother me.

But it does.

God. Why does the man I work for have to be so infuriating sometimes? Wouldn't hurt him to say a bit more.

"Ready!" Willow chirps.

Tucking my phone into my pocket, Willow's bright face greets me. She's now wearing bright purple leggings, a Denver Mountain Lions sweatshirt, and a worn-in pair of hiking boots. It's hard not to smile at how excited she is.

"You are. Let's go."

"Where are we going?" she asks as she climbs into her booster seat and buckles in.

"You don't like surprises, do you?"

She shakes her head. "Only at Christmas and my birthday. Do you like surprises?"

"I love surprises."

I point the car in the direction of the mountains and head out. It's the perfect spring day. Bright blue skies with the first signs of life starting to pop out after a long winter.

"What's the best surprise you've ever gotten?"

"My favorite surprise? I think it's the camera that my dad got for me."

Even though he was trying to buy me off after the divorce, I can't hate it. It introduced me to the one thing in life that will never let me down.

Photography.

And now the chance to make a living with it is so close, I can taste it. Working at the gallery this fall in Seattle is a dream come true.

It's a short drive from Mason's to the trailhead. This early in the spring, even though it's a clear day, it's virtually empty here. A few people are out, but nothing like the summer busy season.

"We're already here?"

Peering into the rearview mirror, I see Willow looking out the window.

"We are. C'mon, Pipsqueak."

Willow, eager for the hike, unbuckles herself and is out the door as soon as the car is parked.

"I don't think Daddy's ever brought me out here."

"Where do you usually go hiking?" Grabbing my camera, I lock the door behind me.

"In the mountains."

"You go inside the mountains? What's it like in there?" I laugh.

"You're silly." Willow links her hand with mine as we head out on the trail. It's an easy one, rolling through the meadows before twisting into the foothills. "I like silly people."

"Me too."

It's a different change of pace, being out here with Willow. Instead of observing everything, taking pictures, we're enjoying ourselves.

"Are you going to be playing with me all year?" Willow asks.

"Only until the end of the summer."

"What's at the end of summer?"

"I'm moving to Seattle."

"Why do you want to move to Seattle?" Willow asks. I love how inquisitive she is. Always asking questions about anything she wants.

"I love art and want to help other people love it too."

"Like coloring?"

"Here, I'll show you." I point to the grasses in the field ahead of us. In the summer, it'll be in full bloom of wild-flowers. "Run through that field toward me, and I'll take your picture."

Willow does exactly as I tell her. Changing the settings,

I snap her picture as she runs to me. Everything but her is out of focus, the grass blowing in the wind. It's the perfect picture with me capturing her big smile.

"Come look." I kneel down, showing her the picture through the tiny digital screen.

"How'd you do that?"

"A lot of practice."

"That's really pretty. Can I try?"

"Of course. Let's find something you can take a picture of."

"That bee!" Willow points to a bumblebee that lands on a stray branch up ahead.

"Okay." Getting the right settings, I hold the camera and position it in front of her face.

"He's so big!"

Her face is lit up with excitement.

It's one of the many reasons I love photography. Seeing these kind of reactions from people fills me with so much joy. It's why I want to pursue art.

"Press on the button here,"—I move her hand to the shutter release—"and it'll take it."

The camera clicks and captures what she found.

"Can I learn how to do this?" She's staring down at the picture she took. "Can I keep this?"

"I can show you how to do it if you want." I sling the camera over my neck and grab Willow's hand to start our hike. "And I'll print your picture off just for you."

"Thanks, Ivy."

Willow gives me a hug before running up the trail. It's only been a week and I'm already attached to this little girl.

When I came back to Dixon after graduating, I figured I'd be spending most of the time planning my move or hanging out with Gemma. It would have made things easier for me. Give me a clean break from Dixon when I leave at the end of the summer.

One week.

That's all it took for Willow to worm her way inside and make it that much harder on me to leave when the summer is over.

Seattle is the dream.

I just have to keep telling myself that to make it easier. Because it's what I've always wanted.

Right?

Chapter Seven

MASON

"Willow. C'mon. We don't want to be late for dinner."

I swear, I spend half my life waiting on this girl.

"Coming, Daddy." Her voice carries from her end of the house. Daisy runs out ahead of her, wearing Willow's latest creation. It looks like some kind of hat. "Daisy wasn't ready."

"Maybe next time you can worry about you and not Daisy." I quirk an eyebrow at her, but all it gets me is an eye roll.

"Daisy needs to look nice for dinner too." The duh in her voice is implied.

Damn. I must be losing my touch.

"Well, you both look nice even though you don't have to dress up."

Not that I'd call Willow dressed up. I don't fight my daughter on much. I let her be who she is. And that extends to her sense of style.

If she wants to wear a skirt with jeans under it and her winter boots, I let her. Who's it going to hurt?

"I couldn't find my paintings I made everyone. Ivy helped me with them." She hands me the stack of papers as she and Daisy hop up into the truck.

"They look great."

"You didn't look at them."

I hold them in front of my face so I can't see her. "Of course I did. This one is of you, Daisy, and Aunt Layla."

"How'd you know?" She grabs them from my hands as I shut the door.

I run around to my side of the truck and hop in. "Magical dad powers, kid."

"Do you think Aunt Layla is going to like it?"

"Of course she is. You're her favorite."

"Are you sure Daisy isn't her favorite?" Willow asks.

"Why would Daisy be her favorite?"

"Daisy is my favorite."

"I'm not your favorite?" I gasp. "I thought I was the automatic favorite as your dad."

Willow giggles as I head toward the ranch. "Actually, Ivy is my favorite."

I fight the groan, because of course she is. Not that Willow has any idea the hold this woman has over me.

It's hard to be in the same room with her and not fall under her spell. It's the reason I didn't want to hire her. I didn't want to be around her.

I shouldn't be falling for my little sister's best friend.

I shouldn't be falling for someone ten years younger than I am.

Hell, I shouldn't be falling for my kid's nanny.

But here we are.

Every time I'm around her, I need to leave. Not only does my brain react to her, but my body does too.

The last thing I need is to scare her away with a hard-on.

"You're having fun with Ivy?" I ask Willow.

"She does whatever I want to. And she is showing me how to take pictures and lets me help make lunch."

"That sounds like a really fun time."

"I even like broccoli now."

"I'm sorry, what? You hate broccoli."

My gaze flits back to her before turning back to the road.

"Uh-uh. Broccoli is good."

"Since when?"

Why am I arguing with my seven-year-old about broccoli? Such is life as a dad.

"Ivy made it and I liked it."

"I'm glad you did. I think Gemma was going to make some tonight for dinner."

"Is it Ivy's kind?"

"It's broccoli. If you like Ivy's, you should like Gemma's."

"What if they're different?"

"I promise, you'll like it."

I can see Willow shaking her head at me out of the corner of my eye. "I don't like a lot of what you make, Daddy."

"Ouch!" I turn onto the long drive that leads up to the ranch and Gramps's house. Every good memory I have is from here.

There's nowhere else I would rather be than here.

Pine trees tower over the paved drive that eventually turns to gravel as we turn off the main road. I roll the windows down, letting Daisy's head hang out, breathing in the fresh mountain air.

Based on the number of cars, we're the last people here. It doesn't surprise me. Trying to wrangle Willow, who is more concerned with Daisy most days, isn't the easiest thing in the world.

Gramps is rocking on the front porch as I pull in behind Gemma and park the truck.

"Hi Gramps!" Willow calls through the open window, unbuckling herself and then jumping out of the truck. Daisy follows her.

"There's my favorite girl."

She snickers as she runs up to him and jumps in his lap.

"Hey! I thought we were the favorites." Layla opens the front door, coming out onto the porch, two beers in hand.

"You were my favorite when you were this age." Gramps is all smiles.

"You're my favorite, Aunt Layla."

"That's my girl." She hands me a beer and high-fives Willow.

"I even made a painting for you," she chirps. "Did you get it, Daddy?"

"You had them in the back seat with you."

"Can you get them?" She stares up at me with big brown eyes.

Brown eyes I can never say no to.

"Fine."

"You're such a sucker." Layla laughs.

"You're the exact same way." I sip on my beer as I go to grab the drawings. Peter, Nash, and Gemma are now out on the porch.

"Way to be late for dinner, Mason." Peter punches my arm in way of greeting.

I subtly flip him the bird. "Doesn't look like we're late because we're not actually eating."

"Aunt Gemma! Can we have broccoli tonight?"

"Broccoli? Since when do you like broccoli?"

Willow launches into her newfound love of the green trees to Gemma while I peek my head inside, looking for Logan.

"He didn't want to come tonight." Peter knows exactly what I am doing.

"Is his leg bothering him?"

Nash shakes his head. "If it is, he didn't tell us. I don't think he was in the mood for a big Winchester affair tonight."

"We'll take him leftovers," Peter tells me.

"I wasn't actually worried he wasn't eating."

"You've done nothing *but* worry about him since he got back. It's a little smothering actually." Peter sips his beer, staring me down.

"Fuck off. How can I be smothering when he's not here?"

"Mason, you're our big brother. Don't act like you don't worry about us." Layla pats me on the chest as she waltzes into the house. I follow behind her. Willow is content telling Gramps and Gemma about her latest adventures with Ivy.

"Would you like to be the oldest then, Layla?"

"Oh, hell no. I don't need any more responsibility."

"Any word on if you'll get the new storefront?" Peter asks.

With Layla's growing store—handmade clothes and other things I don't wish to think about—she's been fighting the town council to get a bigger space.

"If the dickhead mayor would approve the permits, it'd be fine."

"I don't know what you ever saw in him."

"Hence why I am no longer married to Dixon's mayor. I know he has a problem with me selling lingerie in my store."

"Eww," Peter and I say at the same time.

"Oh, grow up." Layla rolls her eyes and hands me a salad. "Go set the table."

"You two are such babies about things." Nash follows us into the dining room.

For a family as big as ours, Gramps's house is small. With our dad and aunt growing up, it was cozy. Now, when all eight of us are together, it's cramped.

The dining room backs up into a well worn-in living room. Couches dominate the space. A TV hangs above the fireplace. Every Winchester family memory covers the walls. Even some of Willow's paintings have made the cut.

"Daddy!" Willow bursts into the house, screen door slamming behind her. "Aunt Gemma said I could go on a girls' date with her and Ivy!"

"She what?" My eyes find my sister as she comes into the house with Gramps.

"Ivy and I are having lunch tomorrow. I figure if you're going to be working, we could all hang out."

"Wait, do I get to come?" Layla comes into the dining room, a heaping casserole dish in her hands.

"Can she?" Willow bounces over to Gemma.

"If she doesn't have to work, she can."

"I own my own store. If I can't get away for lunch with my favorite niece, what good am I?" Layla looks just as excited as Willow.

"Yes! I get to be one of the big girls." Willow runs over to Daisy, who is lying under the table waiting for scraps. "You have to stay at home, okay? I promise I'll take you for a walk after."

"Why is your daughter so perfect?" Peter asks.

"Because she's mine."

He bursts out laughing, smacking me in the stomach. "Please. If that were true, she'd be grumpy all the time."

"Hey. I'm not grumpy."

Peter gives me a deadpan stare. "You yelled at the delivery guy yesterday."

I point a finger in his face. "I didn't yell. He delivered the wrong bottles to us. You try figuring it out when the kid was high as a kite."

"I never remember people getting this stoned when I was a kid," Nash says, taking a seat at the table. Everyone else follows.

"What's getting stoned, Uncle Nash?"

"Uhh…" He looks to me.

"Nope, that's all you. It's why you should watch what you say in front of her." I lean back in my chair, the weight creaking underneath me. For once, I like not having to answer all of my daughter's questions. Especially one like that.

"You cuss all the time!" He's affronted. "And you're telling me to watch what I say?"

"Daddy says adults can cuss because they're adults. It's also why they get to eat whatever they want."

Everyone at the table bursts out laughing at Willow's words. My daughter really is the fucking best.

"Why don't we all start eating instead?" Gramps cuts into the conversation before Nash can argue anymore.

"I'm starving," Willow whines.

"Here's some of this broccoli you love so much." Gemma scoops a spoonful onto her plate, and she doesn't wait before stabbing one onto her fork and taking a huge bite.

"Willow. Slow down."

She nods at me, both cheeks puffed out, before swallowing.

"Tastes just like Ivy's. I can't wait to tell her tomorrow."

I can't help but wish it were me and Ivy going to lunch tomorrow. After spending the night together and sleeping in together.

God damn it. This is the last thing I need.

I can't escape the woman that is consuming my every thought. Even when she's not here, she's all I can think about.

Sporting a hard-on for your daughter's nanny is the last thing anyone needs.

Only a few more months.

A few more months and she's gone and I don't have to think about her again.

Easy.

Chapter Eight

MASON

A warm hand slides inside my boxers.

"You like that?"

"Feels so good," I moan, shifting into the touch.

The hand strokes up and down, brushing over the sensitive head. A warm mouth closes over the tip.

"Fuuuck."

My hand twists into the soft brown hair on her head. Guiding her as she moves down my hardened shaft.

Her tongue is magic, licking and sucking as she takes me to the back of her throat.

"I'm so close."

She does that thing with her tongue again, swirling it around the tip, and I know I'm a goner.

"Damn, Ivy. That feels incredible."

Right before I come, I shoot out of bed, startling myself awake.

Holy shit.

I just had a sex dream about Ivy.

Shit. It's still dark outside. The house is quiet.

Thank God.

My dick is so painfully hard that if I don't take care of it, I'll have blue balls for the next month.

Throwing off the comforter, I head into the bathroom and start the shower. Stripping down, I step under the warm stream of water.

Taking my cock in hand, I give it a long, slow stroke.

Damn. It feels good.

My life has been nothing but chaotic lately. Even jacking off is something I haven't been able to do. I haven't had a minute to myself in ages.

Water sluices down my chest as I get closer and closer. My balls draw up tight, trying to picture any other woman on their knees for me than the one who woke me up.

Don't think of Ivy. Don't think of Ivy.

Except I do.

And I come harder than I have in ages.

Fuck. It felt so damn good. It's hard not to imagine how good Ivy would feel on her knees for me in real life.

Cleaning up, I turn the shower off and towel off quickly.

I know I don't have long until everything else demands my attention. Even though everything I have to do today is starting to claw its way into my brain, the tension isn't overwhelming me.

For the first time in a long while, I feel relaxed.

Shit. Maybe I need to get laid.

Except the only person who comes to mind is Ivy. And that isn't going to happen.

After I get Willow fed, she spends the morning playing in her room, giving me the chance to enjoy a cup of coffee.

A hot cup of coffee for once.

"I'm bored." Willow flops dramatically down on the couch next to me.

"How are you bored? You spent the night at Aunt Gemma's and had fun with her before you came home."

"Yeah, but that was last night, Daddy. I'm bored today."

Seven-year-olds. Always hitting you with logic you don't want.

"Want to go for a hike?"

She shakes her head, her curls bouncing around. "No. Ivy and I went hiking last week."

"That was last week," I say, throwing her earlier argument back at her.

"I don't want to."

"How about—" The doorbell cuts off any other ideas.

Willow runs and opens it before I can get there. "Ivy! What are you doing here?"

She wraps her in a hug.

"You left your jacket in my car, and I thought you might need it." She beams down at Willow.

Fuck. Every dirty image I had of her rushes back into my mind. So much for not thinking about her like that.

"I'm bored," Willow tells Ivy.

"You're bored? How can you be bored?" Ivy's gaze flits to mine for a split second before returning to Willow's.

"Because Daddy doesn't want to do anything."

"Hey! You didn't like my idea." Arguing with my daughter will get me nowhere.

Willow pulls Ivy down to her level. "He mentioned hiking, but we went last week," she whispers, covering her mouth like I can't hear her.

Ivy visibly shudders. "Maybe you could go to a different place."

"But I like our place."

"I can take you somewhere cool to hike," I interrupt.

"Daddy. I said no to hiking." Willow's hands are on

her hips, attitude present. "Besides, Ivy is going to take me next week, and we're going to take some more pictures."

I love how Ivy is including Willow in the things she likes doing. I can only teach her so many things, and it's good for her to expand her horizons.

"Okay, fine. No hiking. But you can't be bored on a nice spring day. How about we go into Jackson?" I offer instead.

This lights Willow up. "Can we get ice cream?"

"You're going to turn into an ice cream sundae with how much you eat, Pipsqueak."

"But I love it!" she whines.

"I'll just drop this off and get going." Ivy sets Willow's coat on the table, but not before Willow grabs her hand.

"Can Ivy come too?"

I shake my head. "I'm sure Ivy has other things she wants to be doing on a Saturday."

Willow turns those big brown eyes on Ivy. It's the look that usually gets her anything from anybody. Not me. Usually. Only some of the time.

"Ivy, can you please come to Jackson with us? I know I won't get bored if you're there."

Ivy's blue eyes light up. "I have an even better idea. How about we get ice cream and do the Cowboy Coaster?"

"What's the Cowboy Coaster?"

"You've never taken her, Mason?" Ivy tsks at me. "Then I am definitely joining you today."

"Yay!" Willow throws her arms around Ivy again. "I'll go put on my shoes."

"You know you don't have to come," I tell Ivy as soon as Willow is out of earshot.

The last thing I want to be doing is spending an afternoon with the woman who is consuming all of my thoughts.

Waking and asleep.

Ivy takes a step closer to me. "You don't want me to come with you?"

I shake my head, doing my best to ignore how good this woman smells. And how there's a flirty smile playing on the corner of those gorgeous lips. "It's not that. I just don't want you to feel like you have to come. Willow will be just fine if it's the two of us."

"I'm perfectly capable of making my own decisions, Mason."

"Ready!" Willow blows into the entryway, shoes on and a sweatshirt dangling from her hand.

Ivy grabs her hand, smiling at me. "Then let's get going."

God damn it.

It's taking everything I have not to act on my feelings for this woman. And now? Now it just got infinitely harder.

"It looks really high." Willow slinks farther behind me as we wait in line at the roller coaster.

"Look at all the kids coming off. They're smiling." I point to the end of the ride. "I promise, you'll love it."

"What if I get scared while I'm on it?" Willow whispers into my pants.

Ivy drops down to her level. "You won't be riding by yourself. Daddy will be with you, and you can have him go as slow as you want."

"Really?" Willow pops her head out to look at Ivy.

She nods. "Really. And if you get scared, you can always hold on to Daddy too."

Willow looks between Ivy and me, her face showing a little more determination. "Will you ride with me, Ivy?"

Ivy holds out her hand. "Absolutely."

"Will you be okay, Daddy?"

I smile down at her. "I'll be just fine, Pipsqueak."

Walking up to the booth, I get tickets for the three of us. Willow is chatting Ivy's ear off.

Ivy's asking all the questions, encouraging Willow and treating her like they're friends.

Once I saw the two of them together, it was an easy decision to hire Ivy. Willow loves most people. But her chattering can drive even the most levelheaded people crazy once in a while.

And it only semi drives me crazy having Ivy in my space.

Fuck.

Maybe if I keep telling myself all the reasons it's a bad idea, it'll cool the lust I feel toward her.

"Bro. You're next."

Ivy and Willow are smiling from their seats in the ride as the high school kid takes my ticket and directs me to one of the cars. I tuck my long legs in as an older guy makes sure the bar is tight across my lap.

"You'll do great, Willow!" I call up to her.

She's holding on to Ivy's legs as we head up the mountain.

It's a slow ride up as we meander up. Nothing over-the-top. As the crest starts to come into view, Willow's hands get tighter around Ivy.

I know she's in good hands, but it still makes me anxious I'm not with her.

"Here we go!" Ivy yells as we tip over the edge of the track and start a slow cruise down.

It doesn't take long before Willow's laugh hits me. She's giddy as we coast back and forth across the face of the mountain. A few dips here and there, but nothing crazy.

It's perfect for Willow.

As the ride finally comes to a stop, Willow and Ivy are hugging as I unfold myself from the tiny seat.

"Daddy! That was so much fun!" Willow leaps into my arms.

"Yeah? You liked it?" I hug her to me.

Ivy's watching the two of us, a smile on her face.

"I wasn't scared at all! We went so fast."

"You did great."

Willow hops out of my arms and runs to grab Ivy's hand. "Can we get ice cream now?"

"What kind do you want?" I grab Willow's other hand and start the walk over to the town square.

"How many scoops can I get?" Willow asks, swinging both of our arms.

"Two."

"Two?" she whines.

"You don't want to get sick before dinner," Ivy tells her.

"Are we having broccoli?"

"How did you get my kid to start eating broccoli?"

Ivy's eyes meet my own as we stop at a crosswalk. "It's my own special trick."

"I can't get this one to eat anything. I'm glad I have you."

Ivy's bright eyes widen slightly, the sun reflecting in them.

The light changes before I can say anything, and we cross over to the town square.

Way to make an idiot out of yourself.

"Why are there antlers here?" Willow asks as we pass under one of the arches that line the town square.

"You know all the elk that roam around on the ranch?"

"Uh-huh."

Ivy's eyes are glued to mine as we come to a stop in front of the ice cream shop.

"They lose their antlers in the spring and they use them for this."

"How do you know that?" Willow asks, stepping up to the counter.

"Daddies know things."

"Is that the answer you always give her?" Ivy asks, leaning next to me. Her warmth spreads through me at the slightest brush of her arm against mine.

I smile down at her. "Of course. Have to keep the mystique that I'm the greatest dad ever."

"Willow would think that even if you didn't have all the answers."

"You think so?" I ask.

She nods. "That girl thinks you hung the moon. No matter how much she says everyone else is her favorite."

I want to puff out my chest at her words. I shouldn't want to, but I do.

Ivy sees me at my worst. So those words mean more to me than she could ever know.

"What will it be?" the kid behind the counter asks.

"Mint chip and rocky road with sprinkles, please!" Willow gives her order.

Ivy follows suit, and I give my order. Willow and Ivy collect their cones from the woman working behind the counter as I hand over the money.

"What a beautiful family you have." The older woman hands me my change.

All I can do is smile my thanks. Because honestly? Today has been the perfect day.

I wish the three of us could have more days like this. But Ivy isn't ours.

No matter how much I wish she could be.

Chapter Nine

MASON

Finally.

A night of peace all to myself. No unicorns to watch on TV or hearing about how Ivy is the coolest person in the world.

I can finally quiet my brain.

All week—all damn week—I've been trying to avoid Ivy if at all possible. Kind of hard to do when she's the one watching my kid, but the less I'm around her the better.

After we spent the day together with Willow, I was feeling too many things. Things I have no right to be feeling.

I push my arms up, doing another set. The one place I can shut my brain down is at the gym. Otherwise, it's filled with glitter and rainbows from the seven-year-old that is my entire world.

The one who is completely taken with the nanny I hired for the next few months.

I push the weights up again, growling as thoughts of Ivy enter my brain.

That smile.

The way her eyes trace over me whenever I enter a room.

Fuck. Could she be feeling the same thing as me?

Damn it. I'm too old to be feeling like a high schooler with a crush. I have a daughter, for fuck's sake. I shouldn't be pining after a woman who is ten years younger than I am.

I drop the weights down on the floor, shaking my arms out. Sweat clings to my skin as my muscles burn from the exertion.

It feels good.

With things picking up at the bar and spending every free minute with Willow, I haven't had much time to myself. I'm thankful Gramps called to have her over tonight and that Ivy dropped her off over there.

I'm also thankful that the gym is one of the only places open past eight in Dixon. That and the Tipsy Cocktail.

Not that I want to be spending my night drinking where I work.

My phone buzzes in my pocket before I can start my next set.

PETER

Fight about to break out at bar. Need help

FUCK ME. If Peter needs my help, there's clearly a problem. Grabbing my towel, I wipe myself down before shoving it back into my bag and dropping it in my truck on the short walk over to the bar.

People are crowded around the small open area at the front of the bar. Gemma is pushing some guy away from two others that Peter and Nash are now escorting out of the bar.

"What the fuck is going on here?" my voice booms around the quiet bar. It's quiet for this time of night, considering how many people are here.

"Mason. What are you doing here?" Ivy sounds surprised to see me.

"Got a text that a fight was about to break out. I was down the street, so I came to help."

"Mason, we've got it taken care of," Peter tells me. "Just a couple of drunk idiots wanting to take them home."

Drunk idiots. If these two were anywhere else, this could've turned out way differently. "What the hell do you two think you're doing?"

My voice is angry as I turn to Gemma.

She rolls her eyes at me. "Mason, we're twenty-three. We're allowed to dance with guys if we want to."

Now that the two guys are gone, everyone is starting to go back to their drinks. People don't care now that the excitement has gone down.

"Not if you're going to start fights."

"Would you relax, Mason?" Ivy tells me. "God, why are you being like this?"

I grind my teeth together, trying to hold back my anger. I'm fuming.

I have no right to Ivy. She's not my girlfriend. She's not even someone who's interested in me. Hell, she's my nanny.

So why the hell am I acting like a possessive idiot?

Ivy.

She looks fucking stunning in a black shirt that dips low, leaving very little to the imagination. With the way her arms are crossed, her cleavage is on full display for me.

Which is the very last thing I need to be thinking about right now.

"I wouldn't have to if you didn't insist on coming out tonight."

"Oh, fuck off, Mason! We weren't doing anything wrong!" Ivy pokes me in the chest.

Gemma and some guy I don't know are whispering next to us.

"You almost got into a fight at a bar." My voice is flat, trying to keep the anger in check.

"Almost, Mason. We're fine. It's not like I can't take care of myself."

"Mason." The guy Gemma's with has his arm around her shoulders. Gemma looks absolutely beat. "I'm taking Gemma home. Will you make sure Ivy gets home?"

Whoever this guy is, he isn't so bad. I nod in his direction.

"Thanks." I shift my eyes to Peter. "Can you maybe not let them drink so much next time?"

"Hey. They're not drunk. You guys just got shitty that they were dancing with other people. Don't blame me," Peter chastises me.

I know I'm being ridiculous and need to rein in my emotions before I piss off everyone here.

"Let's go," I growl. Grabbing the door behind Gemma and her mystery guy, I hold it open for Ivy.

"I can get myself home, thank you very much."

"You drove here?"

"Fuck," Ivy mumbles under her breath. "I dropped my car off at home and took a rideshare."

"I'll take you home."

"I live in the complete opposite direction from you."

"Then spend the night at my place, and I'll take you home in the morning."

I have no idea why I just offered that. The last thing I want is for her to spend the night at my place. Having her within reach of me when she consumes my every thought is not what I need.

"Why would I when you're being like this?"

A smile tries to fight its way to my face.

"Are you always this disagreeable?"

That earns me a smile back. "Only with you."

We're both outside now. The cool spring air wraps around us. I step closer, inhaling that scent of hers that I can't get out of my house.

Blue eyes widen as they stare up at me. The lights from the street reflect back on me. Her tongue darts out to wet her lips.

It's a straight shot to my groin.

"Then spend the night."

It's a dare. A challenge. A need to possess. A simple request that is so loaded with meaning that she can only give me one answer.

"Okay. Lead the way."

I walk past her, taking a deep breath of Ivy-free air. Her heels clack behind me as I cross the street to where my truck is parked in front of the gym.

Walking to her side, I open the door for her.

The smile she gives me is saccharine. "Looks like you're a gentleman after all."

She pulls the door shut behind her as I walk over to my side of the truck.

The drive back to my house is quiet.

I didn't even see them dancing, but it's like I can picture that dick's hands all over her. I have no clue who this fucker is, but I don't want his hands anywhere near Ivy.

"What were you two even doing?" I ask, pulling into

my driveway. The house is dark. Neither of us makes a move to leave.

Why the fuck am I even so mad about this? It's not like Ivy is my girlfriend. I'm acting like a jealous boyfriend who doesn't want his girlfriend going out without him.

Calm down, Mason.

Although, it's rather hard when the thought of Ivy being my girlfriend and the things I'd get to do with her excites me.

"Gem and I always go out together. Why is it such a big deal?" Ivy crosses her arms, shifting in her seat.

"You were about ready to start a fight at the place I work!"

"It wasn't our fault."

"I don't know why I'm arguing with you." I scrub a hand down my face, trying to let go of some of my annoyance.

"Mason." Her warm hand comes down on mine. It sends a zing of electricity shooting through me. My eyes find hers in the dark. The air is charged in the truck. "Why does the thought of me dancing with someone make you so mad?"

"It just does."

"Nope. Not good enough." Ivy leans closer. "You were acting like a child whose toy was stolen. I'm going to need something better."

Moving my arm, I grasp her elbow, pulling her in close. Her eyes widen. The tips of her fingers rub small circles on the inside of my elbow.

"Because, Ivy…"

She groans. "That isn't…"

For the first time tonight, I don't think. I close the distance between us, sealing my mouth over hers. I swallow down her gasp as I give in to what I've been denying myself.

The sweet, sweet taste that is Ivy Connors.

It's even better than I imagined when her tongue swipes against my lips. She tastes like cherries. Fisting my hand in her hair, I tilt her head, getting better access.

How have I lived without her kiss for this long? I deserve a fucking medal for not caving before now. Or a punch to the nuts because how can I ever go back now? Now that I know how good this feels, I don't want to stop.

"Mason."

Ivy pulls back, and I'm ready to dive back in when she climbs over the console and settles into my lap.

My dick is rock-hard underneath her. I don't even try to hide it, swiveling my hips. Pleasure washes over her soft features.

Ivy's hands find their way into my hair. Those long nails of hers scrape my scalp, sending pleasure coursing through me.

"Fuck."

"You feel so good, Mason." Ivy's lips find mine again. This time, it's not rushed.

We take our time. Explore. Nip. Suck.

I kiss my way down her jaw. Her whimpers and moans push me on. Especially when she grinds down onto me when I suck the tender spot behind her ear.

Oh yeah, she likes that.

The vein in her neck is throbbing as I lick down the slope. Nibble on her collarbone.

"Mason…oh my God."

Ivy throws her head back, followed by a loud thump.

"Ouch."

"You okay?"

Ivy nods, a knowing smile on her face.

The heat between us rushes out, the air cooling around us.

"I guess trucks aren't made for fooling around." I clasp the side of her head, bringing her down to me.

Ivy drops her forehead to mine. "I guess not."

Everything in me is telling me to take this woman inside and take her to bed. Hell, I've jacked off enough times to the thought of her. It'd be easy to continue this.

But something stops me.

"You're not having any regrets, are you?" Ivy whispers.

"No."

"Then where'd you go?" Her nose drags along mine before her lips press against the corner of my mouth.

I want to get lost in her again.

"I want to do this again."

"You know this could get very complicated, right?"

Whatever lust I'm still feeling gets a bucket of ice-cold water tossed over it.

Fuck. I'm so wrapped up in this woman that I didn't even think about the complications.

"Willow. And you're leaving at the end of the summer."

"And Gemma is my best friend. She would lose her shit if she found out."

That gets my attention. "Seriously?"

Ivy nods, her face still close to mine. "Do you remember our friend from high school who dated Logan?"

"One of your friends dated Logan?"

She taps a finger on the tip of my nose. "Exactly. Avery said she couldn't be friends with Gem anymore after Logan broke up with her, but then she went and spread horrible rumors about Gemma about what a slut she was and how she was going to steal everyone's boyfriend. Then she convinced Gemma's boyfriend to start dating her, and then they cheated on her together. She was crushed."

"Why don't I remember this?"

"It was right before Willow was born."

"Still. It makes me feel like a shitty brother."

Ivy is still impossibly close. So close I can see everything she's feeling on her face. "Gemma didn't want to worry you. It was hard enough on her losing her friend, then her boyfriend, but to have everyone turn their backs on her was hard. You know how hard it is to recover from something like that in a small town."

I nod, understanding now. "Fucking gossip mill."

"Exactly."

"Fuck."

Why can't things ever be easy?

"Mason." Clasping my face in her hands, Ivy pulls my attention back to her. It's so easy to give it to her. "I want this. But if we do this, it's only temporary. I'm leaving in a few months."

There's something between us. Do I want to take my time and explore what it could be? Yes. Abso-fucking-lutely.

But I know she's leaving for Seattle at the end of the summer.

Do I take what I can get with her? Or end this now before it even starts?

Except, there's no way I want to do the latter. Not when all I want is her.

"A summer fling then. Just you and me. No one else can find out about us."

A smile lights up her face. "That'd be a pretty good way to spend my last summer in Dixon."

Leaning up, I nip at her lips. "Then we better make it worth it."

Canon
EOS
600D
M LENS EF-S 18-55mm 1:3.5-5.6

Chapter Ten

IVY

A summer fling.

Mason's words from the other night keep rolling through my head.

A summer fling.

A fling.

With Mason Winchester.

Butterflies have been ever-present since we kissed.

God, I wanted so much more that night. It was only the two of us. Each day since, I've walked into their house blushing like a schoolgirl. The way Mason quirks his lips at me when I arrive. The way he lingers as he brushes past me.

We haven't made any plans yet—it's too hard with Willow—but I can't wait to be with him. The feel of his hard cock underneath me in the truck had me squirming.

All I want is to feel that inside me. Whenever that does happen, it's going to be good.

So good in fact, that I even had to pull out my vibrator to take care of my needs.

A girl can only hold out for so long.

My dirty thoughts of Mason in the bedroom stay with me all the way to their house. I gulp down the water in my tumbler before going inside, trying to cool my fluttering emotions.

I've gotten good at boxing them away. I did it all the time growing up. I still do it with my parents.

Not thinking about Mason in bed? Piece of cake.

Until he opens the door with his shirt half-buttoned.

Jesus. I want to lick every single one of the abs that are on full display.

"Ivy."

"Are you trying to drive me crazy?" I hiss.

Mason steps to the side, buttoning his black shirt. "I'm running behind."

I smack his chest as I go into the kitchen. Over the last few weeks, I've gotten more comfortable here. It shouldn't surprise me at all that he's running late. It's typical. He's always making sure Willow is taken care of first.

"Ivy!" Willow comes racing into the living room, wrapping her arms around me. "Can we build a fort today?"

"A fort? That sounds awesome."

"Daddy says we're going to have a big storm come through tomorrow, and Daisy and I need somewhere to hide if we get scared."

This sweet girl. Daisy perks up from her bed in the living room but doesn't get up.

"That just means we'll make it the best fort. You won't even hear the storm."

Thank you, Mason mouths to me.

"C'mon, Daisy. Let's go find some blankets and sheets." Willow runs off to her room, Daisy hot on her heels.

Mason tracks her movement. As soon as she clears the hallway, he pulls me into his arms.

"Hi."

"Hi."

His lips are soft, with the faintest hint of coffee and mint lingering there. It's brief, only for a moment, but it has my toes curling and my stomach swooping.

"I wish I didn't have to rush out the door."

"Mmm, yes. I'd hate for you to be even later than usual." My hands trace his well-defined pec muscles.

"I'd hate to make my brother fire me."

"If that were the case, you'd have a lot more free time on your hands."

Those hands of his drift farther down my back, pulling me into him. "More time to spend with you?"

"Yes." I press a kiss into his jaw.

"What a hardship that would be. Maybe I should get myself fired."

"But then how would you support your daughter?"

"Ugh." Mason buries his face in my neck. "Don't be so full of common sense."

"Sorry. I wish you could spend the day with us."

"Ivy! We're ready!" Willow's tiny voice comes from down the hall.

"My charge calls." I smile up at Mason whose gaze seems to be locked on my face. I don't want him to go, but I know he needs to.

"Think you could get away on Saturday night?" he asks.

"As long as you can find a babysitter for Willow."

"She's got a lot of aunts and uncles who need to spend some time with her."

"It's a good thing they love her."

"Ivy! C'mon!" Willow calls again.

"I better go before she comes out here."

Mason dips down, pressing his lips to mine. It's over

before it even gets a chance to start, eliciting a whimper from me.

I want more.

"Saturday," I tell him, stepping out of his space.

"Saturday."

I already can't wait as I head down the hall to Willow's room.

Blankets and sheets are flung all across her room. "I'm ready!" She's standing in the center, with Daisy lying on her bed.

"You are."

"I didn't know what kind we'd need, so I have a sleeping bag and towels too."

"Very smart."

Some days, Willow reminds me so much of Mason, it's uncanny. Other times, I don't know where she gets all her energy.

I think today is nervous energy. Everyone in town has been talking about the storm that's supposed to come. It's all anyone can think about.

"Have you ever built a fort before?"

Willow shakes her head. "I don't think so."

"They're a lot of fun. We'll need the barstools though."

Running out to the kitchen, I grab two of them before going back for the third. Willow's moved the two into place where she wants the fort.

"Is this good?"

"It's perfect."

We laugh and talk about her school as we set the blankets up over the chairs. They're high enough that it makes for the perfect fort.

Once the sheets are done, Willow brings in every toy she could ever want if she gets scared during the storm.

"You know, you need to leave room for you and Daisy."

"I can hold the toys and Daisy. We'll fit." Daisy gives her a big kiss on the cheek, her ever-loving dog.

"Want to get in and try it out?"

"Yes!"

Holding open the "door," Willow sneaks in with Daisy and then I follow.

"This is the coolest fort ever." Her lantern shoots rainbows up on the sheet ceiling we made.

"This is the best one I've ever been in. Even better than camping."

"I like seeing the stars when I camp." Willow looks over at me. "Can you take me camping this summer?"

"We'll have to ask your dad."

Even though I've only been here a few weeks, I love spending any time I can get with Willow. You can never be sad when you're around her. She's the happiest little girl I've ever met.

She wraps her tiny arms around me. "I'm glad you're here, Ivy. I want you to stay forever."

Some days, I wish I could.

If only the next chapter wasn't coming at me faster than I want.

Because staying here in Dixon seems pretty good on a day like today.

Pretty damn good.

Chapter Eleven

MASON

"**D**addy, how bad will the storm be?"

"Thunder and lightning. Some wind. Lots of rain."

It's all anyone in town can focus on right now. If it's anything like they say it is, it's going to be bad. They even let school out early today so buses wouldn't be on the road in the storm. I know Willow is scared, and I want to downplay it for her as much as I can.

"It won't blow over my fort, will it?"

"Your fort will be just fine. You and Daisy can sleep in there. Maybe I'll let you stay up late and watch extra movies."

Excitement grows, her mind now forgetting the storm. "Can I eat ice cream too?"

"What about popcorn?"

"Yes. Daisy loves popcorn too."

Of course she does. If Willow loves it, so does Daisy.

"Remember she can't have people food."

"Popcorn isn't people food."

"Oh yeah?" I get down on her level, giving her my best stern dad face. She giggles at it.

"Gramps said squirrels like popcorn. So it's not people food."

"You shouldn't listen to Gramps so much." Ruffling her hair, I go into the kitchen to start making lunch.

My phone vibrates from its spot on the counter.

PETER

Need some help closing down the bar. Can you help?

FUCK. The last thing I want to do is leave Willow when she's so scared, but I know Peter wouldn't ask if he didn't need the help.

Let me see if Gem can watch Willow

PETER

I owe you

Can you watch Willow for a few hours?

GEMMA

Sure. Bring her over. Is she scared?

WILLOW IS CURRENTLY SITTING on the couch, reading Daisy a book.

> It's coming and going. I owe you

GEMMA

> She won't be scared hanging with her favorite aunt

> Layla's there?

GEMMA

> Jerk

I SMILE, pocketing my phone. It's almost too easy to make fun of my siblings.

I drop down on the couch next to her. "Willow, sweetheart. I need to go help Uncle Peter at the bar."

"What about the storm?" There's panic in her voice.

"I'm going to drop you off with Aunt Gemma, okay?"

"But Daddy, I'm scared." She wraps her tiny arms around me. If I could, I would never leave her.

"I know, Willow. But Uncle Peter needs some help, okay? I promise, I'll be back as soon as I can. She'll take really good care of you."

"Maybe her friend Blake will be there."

"Blake?"

"He's writing a story."

Oh, that guy. The one from the bar. "Is Blake nice?"

"I beat him in shooting arrows!" This gets her excited.

"Well, you're the best there is. You beat me." And I don't even try to let her win. "Go grab your backpack and we'll head over."

THE WIND IS HOWLING as I pull into the back lot of The Tipsy Cocktail. Dark gray clouds have been moving in all afternoon.

I don't get scared of storms, but this has my nerves rising. I know Willow and Gemma are safe at the ranch. Gramps and Logan too.

The one person who's been occupying all my thoughts hasn't messaged me all day. We've barely started this thing between us. I've only kissed her, yet I can't seem to stop myself from shooting off a text to her and checking in.

You okay? Somewhere safe to ride out the storm?

I TAP my phone on my steering wheel. Nervous energy is buzzing through me. It sits, not showing delivered.

Nash comes up and knocks on the glass, startling me.

"Are you just going to sit in your truck all afternoon?"

I open the door when he steps out of the way. "Sorry. Just checking in with people."

"How's Willow doing?" he asks as we head over to the storage area.

"She's with Gemma. She'll be okay."

"We really appreciate you coming. With everyone living so far out of town, we didn't want to risk them getting stuck."

I clap him on the shoulder, seeing everything that needs done. With bottling coming up, we started moving things to the outdoor storage area. It's fenced in, but that's it.

Anything could blow away with the winds they're predicting. Hundreds of vodka bottles? Not an easy thing to clean up.

"Where's Peter?" I ask, grabbing a box and hauling it inside.

"Right here." He slaps me on the back as I set the box down. "Have I told you lately you're my favorite brother?"

I shrug his arm off. "I'm guessing Logan would be the favorite if he was here and could help?"

"Noooo…" Peter laughs.

"He's at home?"

"We're picking him up and staying with Gramps tonight. My generator is down and I don't want to lose power."

"That's good you'll be together."

Between the three of us, we make fast work of moving everything inside. It's a maze of chaos, but at least we won't have to worry about the bar.

"I owe you, Mason. Seriously." Peter wipes a hand over his sweaty brow.

"I'm a good employee." A smile splits my face.

"Good brother."

"Well, this good brother is going to head out."

Nash grabs his coat and tosses Peter his. The two move in perfect sync. It's like they didn't lose any time at all after being apart for so long.

"We'll let you know when we get home."

"Thanks."

The back door blows open, rain now pounding down.

Shit.

Locking up, we all make a mad dash for our trucks.

Once I'm safely tucked away inside, I check my phone again.

An hour has passed with no word from Ivy. The text hasn't even been delivered.

Damn it. Where in the hell could she be?

I want to get home for Willow, but who is there to check on Ivy?

Making what I hope isn't a terrible decision, I point my truck in the direction of Ivy's apartment and call Gramps over my Bluetooth.

"Mason. Everything get done at the bar?"

"Yeah." I blow out a breath, my nerves ratcheting up as the wind howls around the truck. "The three of us made quick work of it."

"You headed to come get Willow?"

"Listen, Gramps. Could you keep her a little longer? I have to check on a friend I haven't heard from. Make sure they're okay."

I'm very careful to make sure I don't say she. No need to get the family gossip trails moving.

"Be careful, okay?"

"I will. But I don't know if I'll make it back over there before the storm hits."

Why the fuck isn't Ivy answering her phone? I know everyone is safe except her.

"I'll keep Willow tonight."

"She's really scared of storms."

Gramps chuckles. "I know she is. I've met my great-granddaughter before. I'll keep her occupied."

"I told her she could watch extra movies and sleep in her fort."

"All things I have. I'll set up the tent in the living room for her."

I blow out an anxious breath. "Thanks, Gramps."

"No thanks needed. It's what family does."

"Call me if you need anything."

"I will."

I hang up the phone. The knot in my chest doesn't get any looser. Hardly anyone is on the road as I slow down in front of Ivy's apartment complex outside of town. Her car isn't in the parking lot.

Shit.

Where in the ever-loving fuck could she be?

The rain comes down harder as I circle the parking lot, checking one last time to see if she's there.

No such luck. I can't stay out in this weather. Maybe by the time I get home, I'll have heard from her.

It feels like hours before I'm finally pulling into my neighborhood. The sky is so dark with clouds it's black as lightning cracks across the sky.

I barely notice because I see the best sight I've seen all afternoon.

Ivy's car in my driveway.

Pulling in beside her, I spot her on the porch. She's soaking wet from the rain blowing straight across.

"Since when do you lock your door?" Ivy shouts over the rain.

"The wind blew it open earlier. I had to lock it."

"Do you mind opening it?"

Water sluices down her face. "Shit, sorry."

I push open the door, letting her go in before slamming it shut behind me. Thunder rattles the walls as lightning cracks across the sky.

"Is Willow okay?" It warms every ounce of me that her first thought is my daughter.

"She's okay. She's staying with Gramps tonight."

"But her fort!"

"She'll sleep in it tomorrow and be fine."

"Why were you even out?" Ivy shrugs out of her rain coat. It's sopping wet.

My words come out mumbled.

"What?" Ivy is breathless.

"I was checking on you."

"You were?" There's a hint of something in her voice. Affection?

"You didn't answer my text. I wanted to make sure you were okay."

"I was hiking and the storm arrived a lot sooner than I thought it would. By the time I got back to my car, it was closer to come here than go home. I figured you wouldn't mind."

Something about her coming here for shelter has my heart swelling in my chest.

I close the distance between the two of us, backing her up against the wall.

"You can always come here, Ivy. Always."

Ivy's lips are on mine before I can even finish the sentence. When our mouths connect, there's more electricity than the lightning outside.

It's fucking explosive.

Her skin is cold from the rain. And I know just the thing to warm her up.

Hoisting her into my arms, I head straight for my bathroom. Ivy's lips kiss and suck a trail up my neck. It's so good, my dick is ready to bust out of my jeans.

Opening the glass door, I turn the shower on, then turn back to face Ivy, who has already pulled her wet shirt and jeans off.

Fuck.

She's in her bra and underwear, and she's even sexier than I could have imagined.

"You just going to look?"

I nod, closing the distance between us. "When you look like this, can you blame me?"

"Maybe a little more touching." When she tilts her head up, her lips look even more inviting.

"Your wish is my command."

Grasping her hips, I pull her in toward me, rubbing my hard length over the softness of the fabric covering her pussy. My hands explore all the naked skin, pulling the straps of her bra down. My mouth sucks and nips on her skin as I push the cups of her bra off her tits.

"Holy shit." Two pieces of metal glint from Ivy's nipples. "Piercings?"

She nods, biting her lip as she backs into the shower, slipping out of her underwear.

I undress faster than I ever thought possible. Ivy looks like a goddess standing under the water, letting it run down her body.

It's the sexiest fucking thing I've ever seen. There's no way I'm not fucking her in there. Grabbing a condom from my bathroom cabinet, I step in, closing the door behind me.

"Looks like someone else looks pretty good naked."

I growl, spinning us to block the water from getting in her eyes.

Her lips connect with mine again. Her nails claw down my chest as I take one of her nipples between my fingers. "These are so fucking hot."

"Gah!" she moans, arching into my touch. "They feel really fucking good, too, when you play with them."

"Is that a request?" Tilting her head back, I make her eyes meet mine.

"If you want." She shrugs a slender shoulder.

"If I want…" Bending down, I drag the flat of my

tongue over the hardened peak, swirling it to feel the metal move with it.

"Mason."

The way she says my name—no, moans it—has my dick aching. He's ready to get in on the action. Giving it a slow stroke, I will it to calm down. I want to make this night last.

I want to squeeze every last drop of pleasure I can from Ivy before I take mine.

It seems she has other ideas though as her hand closes around my cock.

"Fuck," I hiss. Her hand looks so good wrapped around me that I have to take a steadying breath to not blow my load.

"I've been imagining this."

"Oh yeah?" I ask, watching as she gives me a slow stroke. The heat billows and swirls around us. I rock into her hold, watching as her hand moves down me.

"I've been imagining this too." Ivy sinks to her knees, and oh fuck. It's exactly like I pictured that day in the shower.

Except a million times better. Her hot mouth engulfs me, blocking out all common sense. I know we should be fast, not showering when it's storming, but right now, all I want is Ivy.

Her slurps and moans as she sucks me down has pleasure building in my balls.

"No way." I pull back. The first time I come is not going to be down her throat. Maybe later. After I've given her many, *many* orgasms.

Grabbing the condom, I roll it down my dick and shut off the water. Carrying her out of the shower stall, I rest her on the ledge of the bathroom counter.

Before I get my dick in on the action, I sink two fingers

inside her tight, wet pussy. I want her nice and stretched out before I push inside.

"Mason." Her fingers dig into my skin, pulling me into her. Each crook of my finger inside her has her squirming, arching into me. I love how responsive she is.

It's so sexy, watching her like this. One of her hands starts to play with her nipple, twisting and pulling.

"I'm ready. Please don't make me wait."

Capturing her mouth with mine, I pull my fingers out and push my cock in her. Slow inch by slow inch.

It's pure bliss. She's tight, squeezing me when I fully seat myself inside.

Ivy swivels her hips, letting me know to move.

I drop my forehead to hers and watch as I slowly pull out and push back inside. My movements are unhurried.

"You look so good. Taking me like this." Ivy's eyes watch as I pump into her. Our bodies are slick as we hold on to each other.

Each squeeze of her pussy is pushing my pleasure to new heights. It's never been this good. Ivy feels fucking amazing as she watches the way I slide inside her. Her eyes are glazed over with lust as I pick up the pace.

"So close. So close, Mason."

I drag my thumb over her clit, my movements becoming less steady and more erratic. When she finally comes, her body stiffens under mine. It only takes a few more pumps before I'm coming inside her.

"Holy shit."

Ivy pulls me close to her, holding on as I stay inside her. Neither one of us wants to move as we come down from our high.

"Holy shit was right," Ivy whispers. Her fingers play with my hair. The slightest touch from her has me wanting to do that all over again.

I pull back, planting a kiss on her. I can't get enough of her mouth.

"Someone's greedy," she whispers.

"Can you blame me?"

Her fingers drag over my face. "We've got all night, Mason."

I'm going to make good use of every last minute with her.

Canon
M LENS EF-S 18-55mm 1:3.5-5.6
EOS
600D

Chapter Twelve

IVY

Rain against the windows wakes me. The skies are gray as the wind howls. A soft voice is quiet next to me.

"I'll see you soon, Pipsqueak. I love you too."

"Everything okay?" I ask, stretching my tired muscles.

"Someone's finally awake." Mason shifts in the bed, his fine body on full display.

"Someone kept me up all night."

"Not the storm?" he asks.

"Was that Willow on the phone?"

He nods. "She's doing fine. Had a sleepover with all her uncles and slept like a baby in a tent in the living room."

"Good." I know she was scared about the storm.

"And how did you sleep, Ivy?"

My mind wanders back to last night. It was better than I ever imagined it could be. And believe me, I'd imagined it.

The way Mason kissed. The way he paid attention to what turned me on. It sends my blood sizzling, even now.

"Never better." I roll over, the sheets tangling around my waist. Mason is wearing a pair of boxers, holding two cups of coffee. "And you?

"Never better," he parrots back. "How you feeling this morning?"

"Sore."

"Do I need to kiss you and make you feel better?" He drops a quick kiss on my lips before going back to his coffee.

"Who knew that many orgasms could wring a girl out?" I take my own sip, loving the service I'm getting from him this morning. I've never had a night like last night. At most, I'd only ever had one good orgasm, maybe two if I was really lucky.

Not with Mason. Oh no. That man took care of my every need. Even some I didn't know I had. The way he learned my body and paid attention isn't something I'm used to.

A cocky smile stretches Mason's gorgeous lips. "You thinking about it right now?" He nips at my jaw.

"Maybe."

"If you need more to test that theory, I'd be happy to oblige."

I smack his bicep. "I might need a bit more rest before that happens."

"So this is happening again?" Mason stretches out beside me, looking so good I could eat him. "No second thoughts after last night?"

Setting the coffee cup down on the nightstand, I snuggle into his side. It feels so good to be with him like this.

"No second thoughts."

"Can I make a confession that might make me seem uncool?"

I roll my eyes. "I don't think you'll seem uncool, but try me."

Resting his elbow on the pillow and his head in his hand, Mason stares down at me. His brown eyes are clear as they focus on me.

I love that he gives me his full attention. It's not wandering or looking at his phone.

It's all on me.

"I've wanted this to happen for a while."

"You have?" That gets my attention.

I've had a crush on Mason for as long as I can remember. I never did anything about it because he always seemed so out of reach. Unattainable.

And now he tells me he's wanted this to happen for a while?

My mind is blown.

"Since when?"

"It was your twenty-first birthday."

I suck in a breath. I remember that day so vividly. Both my parents were in town to celebrate and got into a screaming match about something so mundane at dinner, I can't even remember what it was.

What I do remember?

Mason being outside the restaurant when I was crying about it. All I had wanted was one dinner where they could be civil with each other. It was my birthday, right? They couldn't even give me that.

I felt that hangover for a week after all the shots I did. I've never been a big drinker, but I wanted to forget that night and how they acted and made me feel.

"I hated how sad you looked." He tucks a lock of hair behind my ear. "But you were also so fucking beautiful, that I couldn't piece it together in my head. Why anyone would make you cry like that was so fucked-up."

"You took me inside, bought me a shot, and told me that eventually it'd be okay."

Mason rubs a nervous hand over the back of his neck. "Honestly, I had no fucking clue what to say. I figured the shot couldn't hurt."

My laugh comes out a bit watery, not quite sad. "I think that's why you made me feel better. Not that I'd be fine, but eventually."

Mason's strong hand cups my cheek, his thumb brushing over my lips. "And are you?"

I shift closer into his touch. One night with this man and I'm already yearning for his touch. His warmth. "Am I what?"

"Okay?"

"Yeah, Mason. I'm okay."

So much better than okay. His words, the way he remembers that night, send butterflies exploding through my stomach.

To hear that the man I've always wanted wants me back? It makes me want to curl up with him and not leave the cocoon we have in his room.

I know it's not possible, but I want it. I want to burrow myself in with this man and never leave.

One night and I'm hooked. One night, and I don't know if it'll ever be enough.

But it'll have to be. I'll have to make the most of this summer with Mason. With one night here and there.

Because it's all we'll get before I leave.

I'll just need to make the most of them with what little time we have.

Chapter Thirteen

MASON

Dinner. Check.

Drinks. Check.

Condoms—just in case. Check.

Everything is perfect for tonight. Our options are limited with Ivy not wanting Gemma to find out about this thing between us. It pretty much guarantees her place or mine.

Because we can't go anywhere in Dixon. Those old hens would have the gossip mill running before we even got out of the truck.

Fucking small towns. Love 'em and hate 'em.

The doorbell rings throughout the house. A swarm of nerves swoops into my belly. Fuck. I can't remember the last time I was nervous to go out with a girl.

Maybe it's because of Willow and never wanting anything serious when she was little. Ivy was dead set on this being a summer fling.

Which is fine.

I don't want anything serious. Serious brings complications into my life that I'm not looking for.

Willow is my priority. Always has been, always will be. Sucking in a breath, I swing open the door.

Fuck.

Summer fling.

It's really hard to remember that when Ivy is looking sexy as sin. A black top hangs off her shoulders, her cleavage on full display. Her nose ring glints in the porch light. And those jeans? Fuck.

She looks like a walking wet dream.

One I wouldn't mind becoming a reality.

"You going to stand there staring at me all night, or let me in?" A smirk plays on the corner of her lips.

Stepping aside, I let her in. Not before stopping her with a hand to her stomach.

Fuck. She even smells delicious. That woodsy scent goes straight to my cock, making him stand up and take notice.

"You look fucking gorgeous, Ivy," I whisper into her ear.

A soft whimper escapes her lips.

Oh yeah. Those condoms will definitely come in handy tonight.

Ivy tilts her head up. I don't miss the shameless way her eyes rake over me. "Looking pretty good yourself, Mason."

I smile down at her. Nothing about what I put on tonight is over-the-top. It's just not who I am.

I'm a simple guy. So I went with a simple white tee and jeans.

But it's the tee that shows off all my muscles.

She breaks free of my hold and walks into the kitchen. Her heels click on the floor. Every bit of this woman is delectable. I want her wrapped around me in nothing but those heels.

"Mason?" Ivy's voice breaks me out of my thoughts.

Get it together, you idiot.

"I'm glad you could come over tonight," I say as I brush a lock of hair off her neck. Goose bumps break out over her skin.

"Me too." She leans farther into my touch. "Where's Willow?"

"Hanging out with her favorite aunts tonight."

Ivy smiles. It's genuine. One she always has when talking about Willow.

One of the many reasons I knew she'd be perfect for this job.

"I'm sure they're eating ice cream and watching all her favorite movies by now."

Laughter burbles out of me. "That girl eats way too much ice cream."

"Maybe if you didn't spoil her."

"Like you don't?" I quirk a brow down at her, stepping into her space.

I've got a solid foot on Ivy. Yet, she still somehow fits perfectly with me.

"I'm just following your lead."

"Then why don't you follow mine now?" Taking her hand in mine, I pull her outside.

String lights hang from the back deck. Dinner is already on the table with wine poured for her and a beer for me.

"Mason. This looks amazing."

Ivy turns her back to the table, wrapping her arms around my neck. Cupping the back of my neck, she brings my mouth to hers.

She tastes sweet. So sweet. Her tongue brushes against my lips before pulling back.

"Why'd you stop?" I growl.

Fuck dinner. The last thing I want to do is eat dinner. All I want is Ivy.

"There will be more where that came from." Ivy holds her hair back, taking a deep inhale of the food. "I'm guessing you got this from the ranch?"

I scrub a hand over my eyebrow. "What gave it away?"

Ivy's smile does funny things to my insides. It's like the moment we started this thing between us, a switch was flipped.

I'm letting myself take notice of her. The small things she does that I never noticed before are now driving me crazy with need.

"Mason. You are not known for your cooking skills. I tried the mac and cheese you made Willow for dinner last week. It was almost inedible."

"Hey! It wasn't that bad!"

"It's from a box. How do you screw that up?" She takes a seat, reaching for her wine.

I stalk over to her, resting both hands on the arm of the chair, leaning into her space.

"I don't see you cooking that often." I nip at her jaw.

"Because the only request I get is for sandwiches. Nice try." Ivy pushes me off her with a laugh.

Collapsing into my seat, I take my own drink and hold it up to Ivy.

"To tonight."

"Tonight." Her smile is coy as she takes a small sip. "What did the ranch whip up for us?"

"Steak. Is that okay?"

"No mac and cheese?" she asks, smiling as she sips on her wine.

"Do you want me to spank you?"

Ivy's blue eyes darken with lust.

Oh yeah. There will definitely be spanking

"Eat your dinner." She tosses one of the rolls at me as I cut into the steak. Perfectly done.

"I'd rather be eating something else," I mumble.

"Mason Winchester. Is that how you would talk if we were out in public?" Ivy admonishes me.

"You know I can't get enough of you."

She rolls her eyes but kicks her feet up into my lap.

I top off her wine. "Sorry we can't go out."

"It's okay. This is a pretty nice setup you've got here."

The string lights cast Ivy in a golden glow. She's so at ease here, like she doesn't have a care in the world.

She almost looks at home here.

And while I know she's not here for long, I put that out of my mind for tonight.

Tonight? All I will be thinking about is her.

Chapter Fourteen

MASON

"How is that your favorite?" Ivy looks disgusted.

"What's wrong with coffee-flavored ice cream?" I stab my spoon in the softened cream, pulling out a big scoop of the tan stuff.

"It's so boring." She rolls her eyes at me. "Even mint chip is more exciting."

"You sound like Willow."

Ivy points her spoon in my direction.

She's laid out on the couch. With nothing but my T-shirt covering her, she looks sexy as hell. After a few orgasms, we needed some sustenance.

"That kid is smart. Her dad has bad taste."

I set the pint down on the coffee table, pulling Ivy's bare legs over my lap. "Oh, I do?"

She nods, eating a big spoonful. It has my dick hardening in my pants.

"The worst taste imaginable."

"And here I thought I had decent taste."

Ivy sets her own container down next to mine and crawls over on the couch, settling on my lap. "In me? Yes."

Her cool lips come down on my own. She tastes minty fresh. "In ice cream? You might need a lesson or two."

"Oh yeah?" I drag my nose along the throbbing vein in her neck. I love seeing how she reacts to me. "How about a lesson right now?"

The way she wiggles her hips over me? Seeking friction? It's fucking hot as hell.

"What did you have in mind, Mason?"

Mason. Just the way she says my name has me ready to throw her down on this couch and have my way with her. I can't remember the last time any woman elicited this kind of response in me.

I toss her on the couch next to me. "Go wait for me upstairs."

Grasping the back of my neck, Ivy pulls me in for a long and lusty kiss. "You better hurry or I might start without you."

I nip at her lips. "There will be more spanking if that happens."

"Mmm, then maybe I should."

Ivy stands up from the couch, giving me a coy smile before running into my room.

This is so not how I imagined this night to be going.

Did I want sex with her? Absolutely.

I didn't think we couldn't keep our hands off each other.

Each time I came with her was better than the last. At this rate, we'll be out of condoms before the sun comes up.

Grabbing the two containers from the coffee table, I grab the other two that are sitting on the counter. It's one thing that is always fully stocked in our house. I don't waste any time hauling my ass to my room.

I know what's waiting for me.

Shouldering open my door, I find Ivy waiting for me,

sprawled out in all her naked glory on my sheets. My room is an absolute mess after having our way with each other.

Her nipple piercings glint in the low light as her eyes track me.

"What's all this?" She extends her arm to me, pulling me down on the bed next to her. "More dessert?"

My smile is mischievous. "Not for you."

She quirks a brow up at me. "Then why'd you bring it?"

"Figured I could do a taste test. See if I like any other flavors better."

Ivy rubs her legs together. "I see. And how can I be of assistance?"

This time, she knows exactly what I'm thinking. Grabbing one of the containers from me, she drops a dollop of ice cream on her stomach. It slides down the slope toward her belly button as goose bumps break out over her skin.

I drag my tongue along her stomach, licking up the pink cream as it runs down her skin. Ivy is arching into my touch as I suck up every last drop that coats her skin.

"Mmm."

"Like the taste of that?" Ivy's voice is breathless as I drop a kiss down onto a hardened nipple, flicking my tongue across the barbell there.

"You know I do."

"We can add strawberry to the list of what you like then."

I smile, grabbing the container to drop more onto her stomach. "I wonder which I'll like the best."

The next one is white with sprinkles mixed in. I let it soften, watching Ivy squirm as it spreads across her stomach.

Who knew eating ice cream could be so much fun?

As my lips suck up what's on her skin, her fingers spear

through my hair, fisting the long strands on top. Every lick of my tongue on her skin draws another moan out of her.

Licking my lips, I lie on my side next to her. Pleasure is written all across her face.

"How'd that one taste?"

I take her lips in an answering kiss. My tongue dives into her mouth. Tasting. Teasing. Enjoying every swipe, every pass.

"I don't know. What do you think?"

"I might need another try." Ivy links her hands around my neck and pulls our mouths together again.

This time, the kiss is slow. Heated. I nip at her lips. She nips at mine. Her leg hooks over my hips, pulling me down into her. It's like we can't get close enough.

"I've got another one I want to taste." I drop a quick kiss on her lips.

Grabbing the most boring of them, I drop the now melted chocolate ice cream on her stomach. I watch as it slides over her sides, coating her skin.

I savor every lick as I taste her. Every bit of her skin is sugary sweet.

Dragging a finger through what's left, I slide my finger lower. Hooking a leg, I open her up to me, covering her clit. The chocolatey flavor mixed with her wetness has me grinding my own cock into the bed.

I'm ready to be inside her, but I cannot get enough of her. The taste of her mixed with the ice cream on my tongue is something I never knew I needed.

It's fucking delicious.

Now? Now I don't know if I'll ever be able to get enough of it.

"Oh my God, Mason." Ivy is practically humping my face as I sink a finger inside her.

Her pussy is squeezing my finger as I strum my tongue

over the tight bundle of nerves. Moans and whimpers hit my ears as I pump my finger in and out of her. As I flick my tongue over her clit.

Ivy is so damn responsive to me. I eat it up.

"I'm so close, Mason."

My eyes flick up to see her. She's playing with her tits, eyes squeezed shut in pleasure.

God. I love that I can make her feel like this.

Adding a second finger, I go at her harder. I want to taste her release on my tongue.

Every bit of this is downright dirty. We're both a sticky mess, but I don't care. I want everything this woman will give me.

"Mason!" Her shouts echo through the room as she comes apart under my tongue and fingers. I slow my fingers, stroking inside her as she comes down from her high.

"So good." I kiss the inside of her thigh as I pull my fingers out. "So damn sweet, Ivy."

"I love how you say my name."

"Ivy?"

"So damn sexy, Mason."

"Are you ready for more?" Standing, I drop my sweats and pull another condom from my bedside table. Ivy already looks thoroughly fucked.

I fist my hand around my aching cock. He really wants to get inside her.

"Oh yeah." Ivy grabs the condom from my hand and makes a show of rolling it over my hard length.

"Fuck," I hiss. The softest brush of her hands over me has me ready to come.

Ivy pulls me down on top of her. She's a sticky mess as I push inside her. I bury my face in her neck, breathing in her scent.

Deep breaths. I don't want to come. I want to enjoy every minute inside her. I have no idea how long this thing between us will last, but damn it, I'm going to enjoy everything she'll give me.

Pulling out, I push back in, setting a hard pace. Each brush of her nipple rings against my own chest ratchets up my need for her.

Ivy's nails dig into my back, urging me on. Sweat coats my skin as I take everything she's giving me.

Smiling, Ivy holds me to her and flips us over, sinking right back down onto my rock-hard cock. Fuck. She's warm and wet and the way she's moving over me? I'm about ready to lose my damn mind.

"So good, Mason. So good."

Her hips swivel over me each time she rocks down. Her abs contract as she takes me. Light-brown hair spills over her shoulders.

Everything about how she moves is hypnotic. The way she's taking what she wants from me is fucking hot. I'm obsessed with everything this woman does.

"Damn it, Ivy. I'm about ready to come," I growl. I don't want to come before her.

"Then come."

"Not before you."

Ivy stops, settling her hands on my stomach. Her touch is soft as she plays with the lines in my abs.

"I'm in control now, and I say you come first. I want to feel you come inside me before I come."

The fight in her eyes tells me not to argue.

"Then get going." I slap her ass.

"Gah!" She pulses around me.

Who knew my girl likes getting spanked so much?

Ivy starts moving again. Faster. Harder. I let everything

I'm feeling for her wash over me as my balls draw up tight. My spine tingles as my orgasm slams into me.

"Fuck, Ivy!" I hold her down on top of me, thrusting my cock into her. "Oh fuck."

Every single part of my body is aware with need as I pour my release into the condom. Ivy is right there behind me.

Her head is thrown back in pleasure as she rides through her own orgasm. I pull her down on top of me, holding her close. Our chests are heaving, trying to catch our breath after our latest round.

I drag my fingers up and down her back. Her head rests perfectly in the crook of my neck. It's like Ivy Connors was made for me.

She fits into every part of me. It should scare me.

This is a fling.

A summer fling before Ivy moves to Seattle.

We've only been together like this a few times now.

But every time we're together, I want more.

More of Ivy.

More of this closeness.

More of what I'm feeling when I'm with her.

"So what's the verdict?" Her breath ghosts over my skin.

"Verdict?" This woman has turned my brain to mush.

"On the ice cream. Which is your favorite?"

I bark out a laugh. "I'll take any flavor as long as I get to eat it off of you."

Chapter Fifteen

MASON

"Daddy! Daddy!"

Footsteps and clacking claws come down the hallway. Pulling the covers over my head, I'm ready for that ball of energy.

The door to my room bangs open.

"Daddy! Wake up!"

As soon as the bed shifts, I fly up. Willow's happy shrieks fill the room.

"You scared me!"

"I did?" I grab her, tickling her sides. "Were you trying to scare me?"

"I wanted to wake you up!"

"And why's that?"

Willow pushes her hair out of her face before grabbing my face in her hands. "Because it's Daddy and Willow day!"

"Are you excited?" Grabbing her in my arms, I walk out toward the kitchen. Daisy is running happy circles around me.

"Yes. Ivy helped me pick out my outfit yesterday."

"She did, did she?"

I drop Willow in the chair and grab everything to make her breakfast.

Make is a strong word. Pouring cereal into a bowl isn't hard work.

"I wanted to have a special outfit for today so she helped me."

I turn my back so Willow doesn't see my smile. I love the relationship these two have. Yet, at the same time, it makes me sad. Because I know it's temporary. As much as I wish it weren't, I know it is.

Ivy will be leaving us in what feels like a few short weeks. And the sooner I wrap my head around that, the better.

Willow too.

"What are we going to do today?" Willow asks.

I shake Ivy from my thoughts. Today is not about her.

"It's your special day, Pipsqueak. You decide."

I set the bowl in front of her before feeding Daisy.

She thinks, shoveling a bite of cereal into her mouth. Milk dribbles out the sides.

"Can we get our nails done? Aunt Gemma said it's really fun to have someone paint your nails."

"Okay." I don't bat an eye.

"Are you able to get your nails done? You're a boy."

"Of course I can. Daddies can do whatever they want."

"You say that about everything." Willow rolls her eyes at me as I grab my own bowl of cereal.

I'm getting more and more signs of what it'll be like to be living with a teenager. She won't want to do this with me when she's at that age. Makes me cherish these moments of her wanting to spend the day with me whenever I can.

"When you're an adult, you can do whatever you want."

"Can I boss you around?"

"No," I say on a laugh. "That'll never happen."

"Aww, nuts."

"Finish your breakfast and then go get dressed and we can start our special day."

Willow makes her cereal disappear before I can tell her to slow down. She's sliding down the chair and running off to her room with Daisy in her wake.

I slurp down the rest of my breakfast before shooting off a text to Gemma. I haven't the first clue on where to take Willow to get her nails done today.

Heading to my room, I take a quick shower and change into my own clothes. Nothing special like Willow. A black tee and jeans. With spring giving way to summer, it's all I need.

The girl of the hour is waiting for me, ready to go on time for once.

"Do you like my outfit?" Willow is wearing a pair of black sparkly leggings with a white tank top covered in rainbows and her pink cowboy boots. Her jean jacket is thrown over the arm of the couch.

I hold out my arms for her to give me a hug. She comes running immediately. "You are the most beautiful girl I've ever seen."

"You have to say that because you're my daddy," she giggles.

I shake my head. "Nope. It's the truth."

Grabbing her coat, I get my keys and head out to the truck.

"Bye, Daisy!" Willow drops a kiss on her head. "Be good while we're gone. I love you!"

Willow races out the door after giving Daisy her bone.

I follow the directions Gemma texted me to the nail place and find a parking spot. Helping Willow out of the truck, we head into a very busy salon.

"Hi. Can we help you?" a cheerful voice greets me.

"Umm." I am so not in my element here.

"Daddy and I are getting our nails done!" Willow tells her, bouncing up and down with excitement next to me. I wish I had half her energy most days.

"Wonderful. Pick out your colors and we'll bring you back in a minute." She smiles at both of us before helping the women sitting in the seats by the door.

Everyone is staring at me, like they can't believe I'm here. Granted, this wasn't the first place I'd thought I'd find myself this morning, but what Willow wants, Willow gets.

Lifting Willow into my arms, I watch as she pulls out bottles of polish and puts them back. One after the other. They all look the same to me.

"This one!" It's hot pink with sparkles in it.

"That's perfect."

"What about you?"

"What about me?" I raise an eyebrow at her.

"We're getting our nails done. You have to get something."

I don't groan or roll my eyes. Because if this is something my daughter wants to do, I'll do it.

Looks from all these women be damned.

"Why don't you do green? That's your favorite color."

"Perfect, Pipsqueak."

Willow goes back to searching for colors before pulling out a bright green bottle. Of course it's the flashiest one she could find.

The woman waves us over to two tables and has a

booster seat ready for Willow. It makes me like this place even more for paying attention to that little detail.

"Are you two doing anything fun today?" an older woman asks Willow. A man sits down in front of me to do my own hands and doesn't bat an eyelash.

Huh. And here I thought this wouldn't be a common thing.

"Me and Daddy are having a special day today and are doing everything I want to do."

"How fun."

She asks Willow about all of her favorite things. My guy is much quieter, but I don't mind. Not until a voice pulls me away from what's going on.

"Ivy! Hi!" Willow chirps.

Ivy looks stunned to see us. "What are you two doing here?"

"Painting pottery," I deadpan.

Her eyes sparkle with amusement as she turns to me. A smile quirks those beautiful lips of hers. "Funny."

"I wanted to get my nails done and Daddy said we could. He loved the outfit we picked out," Willow pipes up.

Ivy is beaming down at her. "I knew he would." Her gaze flicks to meet mine before returning to Willow's. "You have the best dad."

My heart swells at her words. I know I'm a good dad to Willow. She's the most precious thing I have in my life. But a lot of days, I feel like I'm screwing it up. Ivy's words shouldn't mean so much, but they do.

Because of how important she is to me. She sees me at my worst some days. It settles me in a way I never really knew I needed.

I only wish there was a way to make this thing between us more permanent. But with her leaving, I just don't see how.

"What else are you going to do today?" Ivy asks Willow.

"I don't know." Willow screws up her face in concentration.

"I don't want to interrupt anymore. I just stopped in when I saw you in here on my way to grab a coffee."

Willow's bright eyes turn to me. "Can we get coffee after this?"

"You don't need coffee, Pipsqueak."

"Can I try it?"

I shake my head. "No. Maybe a hot chocolate."

"Yes!"

Ivy's smile is wide as she takes in our exchange. She looks nothing less than spectacular. In a simple tee and jeans, she couldn't look more beautiful if she tried.

It's one of the things I like most about her. She isn't fussy. She puts up with my ever-changing schedule and crazy daughter without batting an eye.

Ivy bops her on the tip of her nose. "Have fun on the rest of your special day, Willow."

"Bye, Ivy!"

"Bye, Willow." She turns to face me. "Mason."

"Ivy." I dip my head in her direction.

What I wouldn't give right now to be able to pull her in my arms and kiss her. She sends a wink in my direction as she leaves the shop.

I watch as the man dips the brush in the thick green polish and paints it over my now smooth nails. I've never thought about doing this—even though Willow comes back with painted nails from her aunts all the time—but I can see myself doing this with her again.

It's relaxing. While I wouldn't get this kind of color every time, it's nice.

"All done." The woman caps the bottle and Willow pulls back her hands to stare in admiration.

"How do mine look?" Willow holds up her hands. Flowers dot every finger on top of the bright pink.

"Beautiful. How about mine?" I hold them up for her to see.

"Beautiful," she parrots back. "This was so much fun!"

"Maybe I can bring you back again."

"You liked it?" Willow hops out of her chair, careful not to mess up her new nails.

"It was more fun with you."

Hell, maybe even next time we could bring Ivy.

Following the woman to the counter, I hand over the money and wait for change. A small calendar with the Dixon Damsels sits there. Our college softball team.

"You have a wonderful daughter." She passes back the change, but I give it back to her.

"Thanks."

Willow is admiring her nails as I open the door for her.

"Hey Willow. Want to see the Damsels play today?"

Her tiny head pops up to look at me as a wall of heat hits us. "Can we get a hot dog for lunch?"

"I'll even let you get cotton candy for dessert."

"Yes!" She wraps her arms around my leg. "I want the pink kind."

"Whatever color you want."

I go to grab her hand, but she yanks it back. "I don't want you to mess up my nails."

Holding up my own green nails, I take a step back in defense. "Sorry. Stay on this side of the sidewalk. We'll walk over to the field."

She skips ahead, happy as can be. I wish every day could be like this with her. But life as a single dad pulls me in every fucking direction. Things aren't always easy, but it makes days like this that much sweeter.

Because I would do anything for my little girl.

It's the perfect day for a game. Buying two tickets for the outfield, I steer Willow toward the grassy area.

"You want a hat?" I ask her, passing the stall selling all the gear.

"Yes!" Her brown eyes light up.

The woman behind the counter gives me a big smile as I hand the hat to Willow. She's been the center of attention today.

It's not crowded as we find a patch of grass to watch the game. Willow kicks off her boots and runs around, playing with some other kids and watching the game.

Hot dogs are eaten. Cotton candy is had.

The crack of the bat against the ball draws everyone's attention as it sails in our direction.

"Catch it!" Willow shouts, running at me.

Based on how fast it's coming, there's no way I can catch it with my bare hands, so I take a few steps back, pulling Willow with me, and let it drop a few feet in front of us.

"Yes!" She grabs it off the ground, holding it up. "Do we get to keep it?"

"Sure do."

"Maybe I could be a baseball player like them when I grow up. They're so cool."

"Whatever you want to be, Pipsqueak."

She snuggles into my side as we watch the rest of the game.

The day goes by in a blink. Anything Willow wants to do, we do it. Grocery shopping. Why? I don't know. But we do it. Getting pies from Mrs. Reynolds. A picnic dinner of fried chicken at home with Daisy.

By the time her bed time rolls around, she's exhausted.

"Did you have fun today?" I ask, tucking her into bed.

Willow sets her ball in front of the picture of her mom on her nightstand. Leaning up, she drops a huge kiss on my cheek.

"Best day ever."

Canon
EOS
600D
LENS EF-S 18-55mm 1:3.5-5.6

Chapter Sixteen

IVY

"A country western bar? Really?" Mason quirks a brow at me.

I point a finger in his face. "No complaining, Winchester. You told me I got to pick what we do tonight."

He takes a step closer, his brown eyes dark as they focus on me and only me. His jaw is covered with stubble. What I wouldn't give to feel that between my legs.

I shake my head clear. This isn't the time for that.

Later. *Hopefully later.*

"What are you thinking, Ivy?"

"What?"

Mason grabs me by the waist, pulling me into him. A single finger follows the pulsing vein down my neck. "Whatever you were thinking has your eyes all wide."

My mouth is dry and my skin is on fire as Mason trails his finger lower, tracing the small pendant that sits on my chest.

How can one small body part make my entire body feel alive?

Stepping closer, Mason's hand flattens against my

chest. It's like we're the only two people in Jackson tonight. The cool summer air does nothing to quell the heat flowing between the two of us.

"Maybe I'll tell you later tonight."

"Fuck, Ivy."

Mason's fingers curl into me. Desire is etched across his face. I'm ready to say screw it and cut this date short and head home to where we can act on this.

But I don't. Stepping back, I breathe in the Mason-free air.

"Not until I get to see you do something else for me first."

The smile on my face is devious as I open the door to Mason's protest. A stale, smoky smell hits me in the face. Bright Christmas lights are strung from the ceiling, casting a rainbow of colors across the dimly lit space.

A band is playing an old country song on the stage as people dance on the open floor.

"It's line dancing night?" Mason grumbles behind me.

I spin, pulling him behind me to one of the open tables at the bar. "The Tilt 'N Spin is my favorite bar."

"This makes me appreciate the no dancing rule that Peter put in place."

My boots stick to the floor as I pull out a chair.

"Are you ever going to let the two of us live that down?"

This earns me a grin. "Probably not. Only you two could manage to find the biggest assholes in Dixon."

"We had it handled."

Mason snorts. "Sure you did."

"Hey. Welcome to Tilt 'N Spin. Can I get you something to drink?" A waiter appears at my side.

"I'll take the Spinner and the Dixon IPA for this guy."

He nods and takes off.

"Ordering for me?" Mason leans closer, his T-shirt stretching over his muscles.

God, why is it everything this man does turns me on? You'd think I was a horny college student after having sex for the first time.

"What can I say? I know what you like."

Mason's foot hooks around the bar of my stool and pulls me closer.

"I like that you pay attention."

Resting my elbow on the table, I drop my chin in my hand. "You're pretty easy to pay attention to."

I don't tell him that I've noticed him for a long time. Ever since I came home from my first semester in college. There was something about Mason that winter. Whether it was seeing him with Willow or the way his muscles flexed as he helped Gemma rearrange her room, I took notice.

He was always on the edges of my life, but now he's front and center.

And from the way his brown eyes are fixed on me, he's paying attention. To me.

I relish it.

The waiter returns, dropping off our drinks.

Grabbing the fruity concoction, I take a long pull, cooling my heated skin.

"How is it?" Mason asks, sipping on his own drink.

"Want a taste?" I hold it out to him.

Mason grabs the drink and sets it on the table, pulling me close to him. His lips take mine in a heated kiss.

A kiss I feel everywhere. Mason's tongue slides along my mouth, demanding entry. There's nothing soft about this kiss as he takes over. A whimper escapes me as he deepens the kiss. It takes everything I have not to climb into his lap. I get swept up in Mason.

Until someone bumps into our table.

Mason pulls back, his lips swollen as one side of his mouth ticks up into a smile. His thumb ghosts over my lips.

"Mmm, delicious."

"What?" A Mason-induced haze has fallen over me.

"Your drink."

I wink, getting my wits about me. "Told you."

We watch as the crowd grows on the dance floor. People are moving to the music. It's everything you'd expect in a bar in a town like Jackson.

The best part? It's not Dixon. No one here knows us.

I can sit and stare at Mason Winchester all night long and not worry about another person seeing.

The band changes tunes, a slow song I love coming on. Setting down my drink, I grab Mason's hand.

"Dance with me?" I ask.

"I hate dancing."

"I could go find someone else to dance with."

"Fuck that." Mason downs the rest of his beer.

"Humor me?" Linking my fingers under my chin, I give Mason the sweetest smile I have.

I don't miss the growl that slips between his lips. Or the shock of electricity that zings up my arm as he takes my hand in his.

My hands collide with the hard planes of his chest as he takes me into his arms. Every part of my body is buzzing with nerves or maybe excitement, I don't know which.

Whatever this thing is with Mason is supposed to be temporary. Fleeting.

A summer fling before I start my job in Seattle.

As his hand wraps around my back, settling just above my ass, it feels anything but temporary.

Everything about this moment is charged.

I'm more wrapped up in Mason Winchester than I ever thought possible.

Rough fingertips trace over my neck. My skin is on fire everywhere he touches.

"I know we just got here, but I can't wait to get you home."

I arch into his touch just before he spins me away from him, eliciting a laugh. "You are the worst."

His smile is bright as he pulls me back in. "Gotta impress you with my moves."

"You know I'm already impressed with your moves."

"Well shit, why am I trying then?" Mason makes like he is going to leave the dance floor, but I pull him back.

"Oh no. You are all mine tonight."

"All yours, huh?" Mason wraps his arms around me again.

"Oh yeah. You're not going anywhere."

Because as long as this man is mine to hold, I'm not going to let go.

Chapter Seventeen

MASON

Fucking finally. My house is in sight. After leaving Jackson, it felt like an eternity to get back to Dixon.

Because all I want to do is have my way with Ivy. I don't know if I've ever felt like this before. I've never had this gnawing desire to be with a woman.

With Ivy? It's constant.

Dancing with her tonight made it even worse. That sexy top and jeans that highlight her every curve make me crazy. I was ready to throw her down in the middle of the bar and fuck her just to relieve an ounce of the lust flowing through my veins for her.

I bring her hand to my lips. "Do you realize that you've been driving me crazy all night?"

"Not as much as you."

Ivy drops her hand to my jeans, cupping my hard length through the denim.

"Fuck." Turning into the driveway, I throw the truck in park and pull Ivy onto my lap. "I bet every guy in that bar tonight was jealous of me."

"Why's that?" Ivy angles her neck, letting me bite at the soft skin there.

"Because I got to dance with you. Feel all these fucking curves under my hands. They were all jealous because I was with you."

Ivy grasps my head between her hands. "I bet all the ladies were jealous of me because I got to be the one going home with you."

Fisting my hands in her hair, I pull her mouth down to mine in a punishing kiss. It's hot and messy and so fucking good, I could get off just like this. Each pass of her tongue over mine ratchets up my need for this woman. I swallow down each moan as she rocks over me.

It's so damn good, I don't know if I'll ever get my fill of her.

"Mason." Ivy breaks the kiss, her hot breath ghosting over my lips. "Inside."

Opening the door, I don't let go of Ivy. I carry her across the short distance to my front door and throw it open. Her lips nip and suck at my own neck, marking me as hers.

Ivy wastes no time, pulling her top off and throwing it over my shoulder. Her tits are right there, no bra.

"Why are these so hot?" I flick my tongue over her piercings, loving how good they feel. "I want to fuck these."

I nip at the tender skin, moving to the other one and paying it the same attention.

"God, that feels so good." Ivy's fingers dig into my hair. My attention doesn't move from her chest. I don't know if I'll ever get enough of these.

"More, Mason. I need more."

"More what?" I growl.

"More of you. Everywhere."

Releasing her legs, I grab the back collar of my shirt and yank it over my head. I don't miss the way Ivy's eyes trail over my abs. Or the way she bites into that plump bottom lip of hers.

Pulling it from her teeth, I suck it between my lips. The faint hint of her drink lingers. It makes my brain fuzzy, tasting how sweet and sinful this woman is.

Her nails trace soft trails over my chest as we back farther into the house, bumping into the entry table.

I spin her in my arms, our gazes colliding in the mirror.

It's almost a surreal experience that we're here.

"Look how fucking sexy you are." I drag one of my hands up her stomach. Tweaking one of her nipples, the barbell glints in the low hallway lights. "You have a body that was made for sinning."

"So what are you waiting for then?" Ivy arches into my touch. Her soft whimpers and moans give me all the encouragement I need.

"Someone's needy." I pop the button open on her jeans and slide the zipper down. Each snick echoes in the quiet hallway.

"I want to feel you inside me. Is that such a bad thing?" Ivy rubs that perfect ass of hers against my cock.

"Hands on the table." I kiss a trail down the notches in her spine. She obeys, popping her ass out.

Dragging her jeans down her legs, I take my time, kissing every inch of skin as I reveal it.

Over the soft curves of her ass.

The tender skin on her thighs.

I want it all. I want to mark every inch of it as mine.

I stop at her knees, wanting her just like this.

Grasping her ass in my hands, I bury my face between

her legs. She's already wet. Wet and needy for me as I run my tongue along her pussy.

"Oh God, Mason."

"Mmm. So fucking good."

Running a finger under her thong, I rip it off. I want nothing between us. I don't stop as I slip my tongue inside her. My free hand goes to her front. Her clit is throbbing as I strum it.

Ivy thrusts back into my face. "Keep doing that." Her body is reacting to everything I'm giving it.

And I fucking love it.

My pace is relentless, not giving her a moment to breathe. Each pass of my tongue, each stroke of my finger, I can feel her getting closer and closer. She's riding my face when I slide my tongue inside her again.

"Yes. Oh fuck yes!" Ivy chants as she starts to come around me. I lick up every drop as she chases her orgasm.

When she comes down from her high, I stand. Ivy looks wrung out as she rests her head on the table.

"What did you do to me?"

Leaning over her, I take her lips in a soft kiss. Her moans are feral as she licks into my mouth, tasting her release.

"There's a lot more where that came from."

"I'm addicted to you." Her words are whispered, but I don't miss them.

I drag a finger down her spine, feeling every ridge. I watch as goose bumps break out over her soft skin. "I can say the same about you."

It's like my hands are moving on their own, tracing over every bit of exposed skin.

Ever since Ivy and I started this thing, it's been like this. It's intense, how much we want each other. No...need each other.

We started this thing because we both wanted casual, but now, it's starting to feel way more than that.

"Are you going to fuck me now?" Ivy's words draw me out of my reverie.

"If that's what you want." I unzip my jeans, pulling out my cock. I'm just as needy for Ivy as she is for me.

"Yes." There's no hesitation in her voice.

Finding my wallet, I grab a condom and roll it over my dick. Ivy looks ready, her body on display for me.

Except I don't give her want she wants. I roll my dick through her wet folds. Fuck, does that ever feel good.

Everything about this woman makes me feel good.

"And you say I'm a tease," she huffs out.

"I want to enjoy this." I roll my hips forward. Her warmth envelops me, making it hard to think.

"I'd enjoy it a hell of a lot more if you were inside me."

I lean over her, running my nose along her neck. Inhaling the sweet scent that is Ivy. "You already came once. That isn't enough to tide you over?"

She rocks back into me. "No."

Fisting her hair in my hand, I slam into her.

"Oh my God, Mason!" Ivy shouts, supporting herself on the table. Her skin is flushed as her face is drawn tight with pleasure. The pulsing of her pussy around my cock makes it hard to think.

I pull her up, turning our gaze so we're both staring into the mirror. Our eyes connect. Ivy's blue eyes are dark with pleasure. "Look how fucking hot we look together."

Pulling out oh so slowly, I slam back inside her.

"Fuck." It's a growl. Every pump of my hips inside this woman increases the connection between us.

Tipping her head back, I run a hand down her chest. Her tits are ripe for the taking as I shift my attention there. "Touch yourself."

Ivy whimpers as she plays with her clit. My hold on her is punishing as we chase our release.

Everything about this moment with Ivy is hot as fuck. Watching the two of us work her body together is mesmerizing. A flush of color rises up her body as she chokes my cock with each punch of my hips inside her.

"I'm gettin' real close, Ivy." I thrust inside her harder. Faster. I'm right there, but I want her to come with me.

"I…I'm…" she trails off.

It only takes a few more pumps of my hips before her body goes lax in my arms as she comes undone.

I hold her to me, furiously chasing my release as her pussy rips it out of me.

"Fuck!" My shout echoes through the empty house. "Oh fuck."

My mind goes blank as I hold myself inside her. Hold Ivy to me.

The world could have ended and I wouldn't have known because the only thing that matters right now is the woman in front of me. The one that I'm holding on to for dear life.

"Mason. That was…wow."

I smile into her neck. "Wow is right."

Our eyes lock in the mirror. Her smile is soft as we stare at each other.

It hits me. I am so far gone for this woman, it's not even funny. I don't want a few nights of casual with her. I want this every chance I can get.

I pull out of her, tying off the condom, and step back.

"You're not going to leave me here like this all night, are you?"

Kicking out of my jeans, I pull Ivy's off.

"Oh no." I sweep her into my arms. "There is plenty

more of that tonight. A whole night with you all to myself."

"Then let's go, Mason. I want you every minute I can get."

Every minute of every day.

If only it were possible.

Canon
EOS
600D
M LENS EF-S 18-55mm 1:3.5-5.6 III

Chapter Eighteen

IVY

"**L**ook at this picture."

Willow holds up a picture of flowers in bloom. Pinks and yellows are in focus in the foreground, while the mountains behind it are out of focus.

Spring gave way to summer. The weeks are passing by in a blur.

Willow. Mason. Days and nights spent with two of my favorite Winchesters, all the while lying to my other favorite.

I hate doing it, but I can't bring myself to stop.

"You are a natural, Willow."

I love getting to teach her all about photography. It's one of my favorite things in the world, and sharing it with her is special.

"Taking pictures is so fun." She holds up another picture of Daisy, her tongue hanging out.

"Hey. Where's my favorite girl?" Mason's voice rings loud as he walks in the door.

"Daddy!" Willow leaps into Mason's open arms.

"You're home early." I set Willow's pictures on the counter.

"It's the county fair tonight. Of course I'm home early."

Willow wiggles out of Mason's arms and runs back to me. "The fair is my favorite, Ivy. I love all the rides."

"What's your favorite?"

"I love the big slide."

"That was my favorite too."

Wide brown eyes stare up at me. "Ivy, will you come with us?"

"I don't know. I don't want to intrude."

"You won't be. I want you to come." Willow holds my hand, pleading with me. "Right, Daddy?"

"I don't know, Willow. Maybe Ivy has other plans."

"She doesn't." Willow runs over to Mason. "She just told me she was going out to take pictures. That's boring."

"Willow. That's not nice," Mason reprimands her.

"I mean, if you don't mind if I tag along, it does sound more fun."

I lock eyes with Mason. A heated look passes through his gaze, gone just as fast. "We'd love to have you."

"Yay!" Willow comes back to me, throwing her arms around me. "This is going to be the best night ever!"

"Go put your shoes on, Pipsqueak."

"We're gonna have so much fun." Willow charges out of the kitchen.

Mason closes the distance between us, tucking a lock of hair behind my ear. His touch lingers, sending shockwaves through me. "And here I thought I wouldn't get to see you much tonight."

This man's mere presence is overwhelming. Every part of my body is tingling from the soft brush of his fingers. Mason is less than a foot from me. Willow's soft voice carries from the other room. I drop a soft kiss on his lips.

"Looks like we will."

"I'm glad I don't have to wait until the weekend to see you."

I hate how fleeting my time with Mason is. In a few short weeks, I'll be heading out to Seattle. Mason's priority is Willow. It makes getting what little time we can that much harder.

The girl in question comes running back into the kitchen. Mason jumps back, slamming his back into the counter.

"Shit!" Mason winces, rubbing at his back.

"I'm ready!" Willow is back at my side, staring her dad down. "What's wrong?"

"Nothing. I'm fine."

I hide the smile as Mason mouths, *your fault.*

"Then let's go."

Grabbing my hand, Willow drags me out of the house. All I can do is pat Mason on the chest as we head out to the truck and get on our way to the fair.

It's the perfect summer night. With the holiday week-end, Dixon is overrun with tourists. Everyone is in town to go hiking at the national park.

I can't blame them. I love the Tetons. They're my favorite. But I like sticking to the trails that only Dixonites know.

They're quieter. Easier for me to get lost in my art.

The fair is only a short ride from Mason's house. It's hard being in a confined space with him like this and not being able to reach over and touch him. Feel his warmth.

The last thing we need is for Willow to find out about the two of us. It's not fair to her when this is only for the summer.

The summer.

It's going by in the blink of an eye. And before I know it, I'll be packing up and heading to Seattle to start my new life.

What I've always wanted.

"There's so many people here," Willow chimes in from the back seat. Mason pulls the truck into an empty spot in the field being used for the fair.

Cars and people are everywhere. Excited voices can be heard over the chimes and music of the carnival rides. A Ferris wheel is set back, drawing everyone's eye to it.

"Make sure you stay by me or Ivy, okay?" Mason turns in his seat, facing Willow.

"Okay, Daddy. Do you think you can win me a goldfish?"

"A goldfish?" I hop out of the truck and open Willow's door, helping her down. "Why do you want a goldfish?"

"Jamie at school got one and she named it Nemo. I want one too."

Mason rolls his eyes as he comes and takes Willow's hand. "We are not getting a goldfish. What if Daisy tried to eat it?"

Willow's eyes go wide as she takes my hand. "Daisy doesn't eat fish. She only likes people food."

"And why would she like people food when we're not supposed to feed her?" Mason eyes me over her head. A playful smile is on his face.

I love that I get this side of him.

To everyone else, he's the surly oldest brother of the Winchester clan. The one people don't want to mess with.

It's all a facade.

Mason has a heart of gold. He loves his people fiercely. The way he is with his daughter turns me into a puddle.

It's what is making this whole *summer only* thing that much harder.

I thought I knew the real Mason.

Turns out, he doesn't hold a candle to the man I've gotten to know.

Mason stops at the ticket booth and buys us each a wristband for unlimited rides. "Any tickets for the games?" the woman asks.

"We'll do two."

"Five!" Willow chimes in.

Mason eyes her. "Three."

"Four." Willow holds up four fingers.

"I guess four."

Wrapped around her little finger.

"Where do you want to start?"

People are everyone. Bright lights flash from games where stuffed animals hang from hooks. Dings and chimes are loud everywhere. Screams from a few of the bigger rides can be heard.

"The Merry-Go-Round." Willow points to it, bouncing up and down with excitement.

"Lead the way, Pipsqueak."

"I want to ride on one of the horses," she tells us as we move through the crowds.

"You can ride on whatever you want."

We get in line as the attendant waves the first group of people on. A cool breeze starts to blow through as the sun dips closer to the horizon.

"What do you want to ride, Ivy?"

Mason crosses his arms, eyeing me. "Yeah, Ivy. What do you want to ride?"

I don't miss the heat behind his eyes.

Damn this man. I want to grab him by the T-shirt and haul him in for a kiss.

But I can't.

And he knows it.

"I'll take whatever is next to you, Willow."

"Yes!" She pumps her little fist. "This is the best night ever."

The ride comes to a stop and the attendant waves us on after the group of people clears off. Mason waves us on ahead of him. Brushing against his chest, I lean up to him. "Keep it PG, Winchester."

His growl behind me has me smiling.

"I want the pink horse!" Willow finds a spot with three horses for us, each a more ridiculous color than hers.

Mason secures her, then swings a leg over his own horse.

"Make sure you hold on tight, okay?" he tells her, reaching over and checking the belt one more time.

"I will."

"Hey!" I grab my phone and pull it out of my pocket. "Smile, you two."

Both of them turn big smiles on me as I snap a photo.

"Take a selfie! I want one with you in it, Ivy!"

Turning the camera, I smile and frame the three of us in the photo. The ride starts and Willow screams in excitement as I click the shutter.

Sticking it back in my pocket, I hold my arms out, screaming right along with Willow. The horses move up and down as the carousel music blasts over the speakers. The fair swirls by in a haze of colors as we spin around.

Willow's screams turn to laughs as she moves up then down. It goes by in a blink. It feels as if the ride has just started when it begins to slow to a stop.

"That was so much fun! Can I see the pictures you took?" Willow asks as I unlatch the buckle and help her down.

I grab my phone, unlock it, and hand it to her. "How do we look?"

Grabbing her by the shoulders, I steer her toward the exit of the ride as Mason follows.

"I love it!" She holds the phone up to me to see. "You can see my pink horse."

The field is a blur behind us as we're in focus. Willow's mouth is wide open and Mason has a smile pasted on his face. My mouth is just as wide as Willow's.

Every one of us is happy.

Mason looks over my shoulder at the photo. "Looks good."

His voice is gruff.

I take the phone from Willow and look at it one last time. There's nothing artful about this photo. It's a little grainy from the movement. I didn't follow the rule of thirds. The colors could be more balanced.

I don't care about any of that.

It's one of my favorite pictures I've ever taken. Because of the two people in it.

"Can we race down the slide now?" Willow asks.

"I'm so going to beat you." I take her hand as she starts to skip toward the towering slides.

Kids are sliding down red, yellow, and blue slides on old potato sacks.

"Not if I beat both of you." Mason runs ahead and grabs three burlap cloths for us.

"I think you're going to lose." I take the one Mason holds out to me.

"Oh, yeah?"

I nod. "The smaller you are, the faster you go."

"That means I'll win," Willow says from between us.

"What if I win?" Mason asks.

"Are you wanting something?"

Willow pokes Mason in the leg. "Hurry up, Daddy! I want a corn dog after this."

I can only laugh at how excited Willow is as she runs up the stairs ahead of us.

"If I win, I want a kiss at the end of the night," I tell Mason as I pass him.

"Pretty sure you were already going to get one." He wiggles his eyebrows at me. "What if I want something else?"

"Hmm. We'll have to see who does win."

We follow Willow up the stairs and wait our turn. As the riders in front of us go, we set our three bags down and take our seats. Mason leans over to Willow, whispering in her ear. She giggles.

"And go!" Willow yells, giving Mason a push before pushing herself down.

"Hey! That's cheating!" I push off and slide my way down.

"You didn't say when we could start!" Mason yells as he races down.

I hold myself forward, trying to gain momentum, but it's too late. Willow slides right past Mason into the finish line, Mason shortly after her and me in third.

"That was so not fair!" I struggle to stand, my legs tangled in the burlap.

"You never said we had to start at the same time." Mason's voice is playful.

"That's the whole point of a race!" This time, I get my feet under me and get in his face. "You cheated, Mason Winchester. Is that really what you want to teach your daughter?"

"We Winchesters like to win!" Willow pipes up.

I give her a mock horrified look. "You too, Willow? You too?"

"Just like her dad." Mason is so proud, it's hard to give him grief.

"Fine. But you're buying the corn dogs." I lean just a bit closer, putting my lips to his ear. "I guess no kiss for you tonight."

"Fuck me." I hear him mumble as I grab Willow's hand and head toward the food stalls.

"You are so sneaky," I tell Willow as we get in line.

"Daddy doesn't like to lose."

"What if I don't like to lose?"

She shakes her head. "Daddy is the worst loser. He gets mad and stomps around. Uncle Peter beat him at Monopoly and he almost threw the board."

"Willow! What'd I say about telling people that story?"

"You didn't lose. Uncle Peter cheated." Willow sounds like she's placating him, like it isn't the first time she's told this story.

"Poor Mason, can't win at Monopoly and has to cheat in a slide race."

"If I want what's on the line, sure," he whispers, rolling his eyes. A smile is still plastered on his face. "I don't know why I agreed to come to the fair tonight."

I drop a soft hand on his chest. "Because you wanted to hang out with the two of us."

Mason's eyes drop to his chest, and I pull back like he burned me.

I know I shouldn't touch him like this. Not in public. Not with Willow around. Not with the prying eyes of Dixon around. But I couldn't help myself. I love getting to be with him like this. See this playful side.

"What'll it be?" The guy in the stall startles me.

"Three corn dogs." Mason grabs his wallet and hands over the cash as I take the corn dogs from the other worker. He drops the change in a tip jar and we walk away.

"Thanks, Daddy." Willow takes her corn dog from my hand and walks over to a bench.

"I love corn dogs." Willow takes an enormous bite.

"Slow down, Pipsqueak. Enjoy it. I don't want you choking."

She swallows down her bite and smiles up at Mason. "I know."

I take a smaller bite, people-watching as the crowd moves around us. People I recognize from school. People I don't. A few workers from the ranch.

It reminds me of what Seattle is going to be like. A chaos of people where I won't know anyone.

It's what I've always wanted.

My mind is distracted the rest of the night as we eat our way through the fair. Ride all the rides. Win Willow a stuffed dinosaur.

"Why don't we go do the Ferris wheel before the fireworks start?" Mason asks.

"Sure."

The ride starts and stops, letting people on.

The three of us fit in one car as it slowly carries us up to the sky. Willow leans against Mason, her eyes starting to drift closed.

"Someone's had a little too much fun."

I smile down at the now sleeping Willow. "I don't think I was ever this excited for the fair."

Mason wraps an arm around me as best he can. "I remember having to watch Logan because he liked to run off without telling anyone. He hated it."

"Such a good big brother."

Mason's fingers play in the strands of my hair as we stop at the top of the ride. The sun is gone now. Colors are splashed across the sky. Pinks and oranges are fading fast as inky blues take over.

"Sometimes I don't feel like it."

"What?" I whip my gaze around to him. "What in the world are you talking about?"

Mason is staring out at the mountains. "I feel like I let my brother down because I wasn't there for him when everything happened."

Logan. It's been a hard few months for the whole family, trying to make sure he's taken care of.

"You couldn't have known that was going to happen."

"But I still wasn't there."

"No one blames you for not being there. You have Willow to worry about. And you've been there for him ever since. You've always been there for your entire family."

Mason's free hand runs through Willow's curls as she continues to sleep.

I continue. "All of my memories when Gemma and I were growing up have you in them. Even though you might not think so, you are an amazing big brother, Mason. And a great father."

Checking to make sure Willow is still asleep, I grasp Mason's chin and pull him in for a kiss. It's soft. Nothing heated or over-the-top, but I try to tell him how I'm feeling about him with it.

He pulls back, cupping my cheek. His thumb is soft as it rubs over my lips. "Thank you, Ivy. I don't know what I'd do without you this summer."

"I should be saying the same to you."

For once in my life, Dixon is where I want to be. Sure, Seattle is there in the back of my mind. It always is. But being here with Mason, with Willow, it's everything I could have ever wanted.

The ride starts again, waking Willow up with it.

"Can we stay for the fireworks, Daddy?" Willow asks around a yawn.

"Of course. What's a fair without fireworks?"

"You hear that, Dino? We can watch the fireworks and then I'm going to introduce you to all your new friends at home."

I smile over at Mason. His eyes are locked on mine. "Sounds like a good plan, Pipsqueak."

Mason easily lifts Willow into his arms as we get off the ride. "This is the best night ever, Daddy. Thanks for coming, Ivy."

I rub a hand down her back. "I've had so much fun with you guys."

She smiles as we follow the crowd to the back of the fair. Willow's already dozing again.

"I'm glad you came." Mason wraps his arm around my shoulders as the fireworks start.

It's dark. No one can see us, or pays us any attention, as colors explode across the sky. Oohs and ahhs are heard as crackles light up the sky.

It's the perfect ending to the night. I want to bottle this up and never forget how I'm feeling. Getting to spend the evening with these two was everything I thought it'd be.

I love being with Mason. He's tender and thoughtful, and even better than I could have imagined.

Love?

Could I possibly be in love with Mason Winchester?

There's no way. We said this would be a summer fling. Nothing serious.

I'll be gone soon.

But as we head back to his truck, I realize I'm not ready to leave.

The ride home is quiet. We're all tired after riding all the rides twice and gorging on funnel cakes. This time, because Willow is asleep, I'm holding Mason's hand as he drives.

I want this little bit of him. Any bit. Because now that I've had that fleeting thought, I don't want to let go of him. Even if I'll be heading home when we get back to Mason's, I'll take any seconds I can with him.

By the time we get back, I'm dozing in the front seat.

"Let me get Willow to bed before you leave?" Mason asks, taking the still sleeping Willow into his arms.

"Sure."

I open the door for him and head into the living room while he goes to her room.

The living room is a mess. Willow and I didn't get a chance to clean up before we left. Evidence of our day—painting, building bricks, dress-up clothes—you name it, it's on the floor. All the photos we've taken together this summer clutter the kitchen counter.

It has emotion clogging my throat.

This is what I missed out on growing up. For as long as I can remember, my parents were always at each other's throats. I spent most days in my room or at Gemma's. I never had this.

Playing. Making messes. Exploring.

No matter how much Mason says he feels like Willow is missing out, she isn't.

That little girl is so loved by everyone she knows, she'll never feel like I am now.

"You okay?" Mason's voice startles me from behind.

"I'm good." I pad quietly over to him, wrapping my arms around him. Breathing him in.

I love that fresh laundry scent. It's all Mason. He can't be bothered with cologne.

"I wish you could stay the night." He squeezes me to him.

"I know. But tonight was pretty perfect already."

"Yeah?" He drops his forehead to mine, his mouth a breath from mine. "Did you have fun?"

I smile against his lips, mimicking Willow's words.

"Best night ever."

Chapter Nineteen

MASON

"Why are you still here?" Peter yells at me from across the office.

"Because the wrong artwork was sent to the canning distributor and it needs to be fixed."

My head feels like it's going to explode. I woke up feeling not great. As the day has gone on, it's gotten even worse.

"You're going to get everyone sick if you stay here."

"Are you going to make sure this gets fixed?"

A coughing fit takes over as it racks my body.

Fuck. That hurt.

"Go home." Peter's standing in front of my desk now, an angry look on his face. "We can manage without you."

"You sure?"

He nods. "Yes. Get better and don't come back until you're one hundred percent."

"Fine," I growl out.

I hate missing work. Especially with a project as impor-tant as the canning of The Clara. It's not something I want to get messed up. I know how much this place and his products mean to Peter.

I don't want to let another one of my siblings down.

I shake the unwelcome thoughts from my head and walk out the back of the bar. For being so hot today, chills run through my body as I jump into my truck.

Fuck.

I really am sick.

The drive home feels like it takes forever today. With the summer season in full swing, tourists have taken over Dixon.

I shouldn't complain, because I know it means the ranch and town are doing well. Today? Today, I am not in the mood for the traffic to be moving slower than a snail's pace as people take in the Tetons.

Pulling closer to the house, I see Ivy and Willow out front, running through the sprinklers with Daisy.

Fuck.

Water droplets cling to every bit of Ivy's skin. A happy smile is on her face as she chases Willow through the spinning water.

Seeing the two of them together like this eases my worry about not being there for Willow this summer. It's been a trying year, what with everything going on with Logan and with Willow's mom so far away. Every night I lay my head on my pillow, I worry if I'm doing enough for my daughter.

If she's happy. If I'm giving her everything I can as a single dad.

It erases my worry seeing them like this. Both of them are happy when they notice me sitting in my truck.

"Daddy! You're home early!" Willow launches herself at me once I close my door. Daisy is happily lying in the wet grass.

"Hey Pipsqueak. I missed you." I set Willow down—not wanting to pass my sickness onto her—and let her go back to playing in the water.

"What are you doing home so early?" Ivy's hands rest on her hips. The black one-piece she's wearing does nothing to hide all those curves I love of hers.

"I was banished. I'm not feeling so great."

Ivy walks over, putting her hand on my forehead. I lean in to the soft touch, loving how her cool skin feels against my own, overheated skin.

Ivy's eyes widen. "You're burning up."

"I feel like shit." Another coughing fit takes over my body. "Sorry."

Ivy takes a few steps back. "Why don't we go inside and I can make you some soup?"

I shake my head. It feels like a lead weight sitting on my shoulders. "I can't ask you to stay."

Ivy crosses her arms, quirking an eyebrow in my direction. It's the face that tells me not to argue with her. "And you plan on taking care of Willow like this?"

Fuck.

The last thing I want is for Willow to get sick because of me.

"I thought so." Ivy spins on her heel. If I wasn't feeling so fucking shitty, I'd admire her ass more. "Willow, Daddy isn't feeling so good, so we're going to go watch a movie, okay?"

"Okay!"

I know Ivy limits her TV time during the day as much as she can, so I know Willow's excited about watching a movie now. "Can we watch the one where the unicorns fight off the bad clouds with rainbows?"

Am I high or sick? That sounds like the weirdest

fucking shit I've ever heard of. But if Willow wants to watch it with Ivy, fine.

"Dry off before you go inside!" Ivy yells after her.

Both of them wrap towels around them as I head inside. Willow's giggles follow as she tries to wipe down Daisy.

I don't even try to make it to my room, choosing to collapse right there on the couch.

Fuck. I must be sicker than I realize because sitting here now feels better than I have all day.

"Willow, once you and Daisy are dry, why don't you two lie on some pillows on the floor so you don't get sick?" Ivy tells her.

"Like our fort?"

"Yes. Exactly like our fort. You can cuddle with Daisy."

Their conversation has my eyes closing. I love how close the two of them have gotten over this summer. It's like Ivy has always been a part of our lives.

To some extent, she has been. She's Gemma's best friend. She's always been around in Dixon for as long as I can remember.

Now, I love getting to see this side of her with Willow. The caring, loving side.

I get the sexy, fun side of Ivy whenever we can squirrel away a few nights. I've loved getting to learn her body and what turns her on.

But I especially love seeing how much she's connected with Willow. I only get a bit of time with them together. The two of them became fast friends before I even realized it.

Willow and Daisy run into the living room, Daisy with a new bone and Willow with a popsicle. She throws pillows on the ground as Ivy turns on the TV for her.

It almost feels like I'm intruding on their special time together.

Ivy's hands run through my hair as her voice gets closer to my ear. "I'll be back with some soup in a few minutes."

I can only nod.

Bright lights and high-pitched voices fill the room as Willow's show starts. The music lures me into sleep.

And the next thing I know? It's dark outside and I'm flat on my back on the couch. The TV is off, and Willow isn't where I last saw her.

I start to sit up, but a hand stops me. "Easy there, Mason."

Ivy's bright blue eyes hover above me. Her face is clean, not a trace of makeup. Her hair is a mess, likely from the sprinklers they played in earlier. Was it earlier? I don't even know what day it is at this point.

"What time is it?" My voice is scratchy and my throat sore.

"Just before seven."

"Where's Willow?" This time, I don't try and get up. If Ivy is here, I know Willow's okay.

"I called Layla to come take her for the night. I didn't want her getting sick. I am under strict instructions to show you the picture she drew you to make you feel better."

"That sounds just like her. Thank you." I close my eyes again, turning into Ivy's warmth. "I can't remember the last time I've felt so crappy."

"I can stay if you want me to." Ivy's hands run through my hair. Based on the way she's touching me, she doesn't really want to leave.

"I don't want to get you sick." I nuzzle against the soft material of her shirt.

It's been so long since I've been held like this. I don't

get sick often, but when I do, it usually hits hard. And I'm the one making sure I get better all on my own.

I've never had anyone to take care of me like this. To hold me when I'm sick. To make me soup.

"C'mon. Let's get you into bed and I'll make you something you can actually eat this time. Maybe even hold you again." I can hear the smile in her voice.

Ivy makes to move, but I wrap an arm around her. "Give me a minute. I want to be yours to hold just a bit longer."

A cool hand comes down on my stomach, pushing up the hem of my shirt. Her fingers rub smooth circles over the flats of my abs.

I breathe her in. It's intoxicating. Her touch. Her smell.

I'd avoided Ivy for so long. First, she'd just been my annoying little sister's best friend. Then I'd realized there was something more to her and I knew I needed to stay away.

Now it's hard to imagine my life without her in it.

"Time to go to your room," Ivy whispers against my forehead. "You're not as hot."

"I've lost hotness? Damn."

"Stop it," she laughs.

Sitting up, Ivy stands and holds out a hand for me. I follow her as she heads down the hallway to my room.

"Lie down. I'll bring you dinner."

I wish I could kiss her right now. I know I'm being selfish wanting her here with me, risking her getting sick, but she hasn't left yet.

As soon as she leaves my room, I pop into the bathroom and turn on the shower. Hopefully a cool, quick one will help clear the sludge in my head.

Who gets sick like this in the middle of summer?

As soon as the water gets warm, I strip down and step under the spray.

Damn. It feels good not to be in those sticky clothes from earlier. Maybe that means I'm sweating out my fever. Even in these last few minutes I'm starting to feel more human.

I let the water slide over me, enjoying the feel of it. As soon as it starts to run cold, I shut it off and step out. Toweling myself off, I drop my towel and head into my room and pull on a fresh pair of boxers.

Even just that bit of movement has me exhausted as I collapse on my bed.

"Feeling any better yet?" Ivy comes into the room with a steaming bowl and crackers on a tray.

"Shower helped." I scoot over, letting her sit next to me.

"Good. Hopefully some soup will too."

Ivy places the tray on the nightstand and hands me the bowl.

"Willow would be mad if she knew we were eating in bed."

Ivy laughs sitting next to me. We're touching from our shoulders to our hips. Even the smallest contact sets my skin on fire.

Even more so than it already is.

"I don't know why kids want to eat in their rooms so much."

I eat a spoonful of the chicken broth. It's bland, but at least I can taste it.

"Trust me, if Willow thought she could get away with it, she would, but Daisy would give it away."

"That dog loves her."

"They are two peas in a pod." I blow on the broth, swallowing another bite. "You're really good with her."

Ivy leans back against the headboard, shifting ever so slightly so she's looking at me. "She's a really good kid, Mason. You've done well raising her."

"Half the time I feel like I'm dropping the ball."

Ivy shakes her head. "Not at all. That girl has the best life there is. I wish I had that kind of childhood."

"If I remember, you were always at the ranch."

A sad looks washes over Ivy's face. "My parents fought my entire childhood. Even when they divorced, they were still fighting. The ranch was my safe place to go."

Reaching across her, I set the bowl down and pull her into my arms. "I'm sorry it was like that for you."

"I'm just glad I had Gemma." There's a note of sadness in her voice. "Which makes this that much harder."

"Do you want to stop?" The words come out more panicked than I intend them to.

There's no way in hell I want to stop. I am so wrapped up in Ivy, I don't know what I would do if she said yes.

"Absolutely not. I just feel like a terrible person for lying to her."

I drop a kiss into her hair. What I really want to do is take her in my arms and kiss her senseless. Remind her of why we're so good together.

Fucking fever.

"She's so wrapped up in Blake, I don't even think she's noticed."

"Noticed what?" I ask.

"That I'm actually happy here for once."

That makes pride swell in my chest. I love being the one that can make her happy like that.

"Then we keep doing this."

"Until the end of summer," Ivy confirms.

Until the end of summer.

Fuck. I don't know what I'm going to do when that comes.

Because there's no way in hell I'll ever be ready to let go of Ivy Connors.

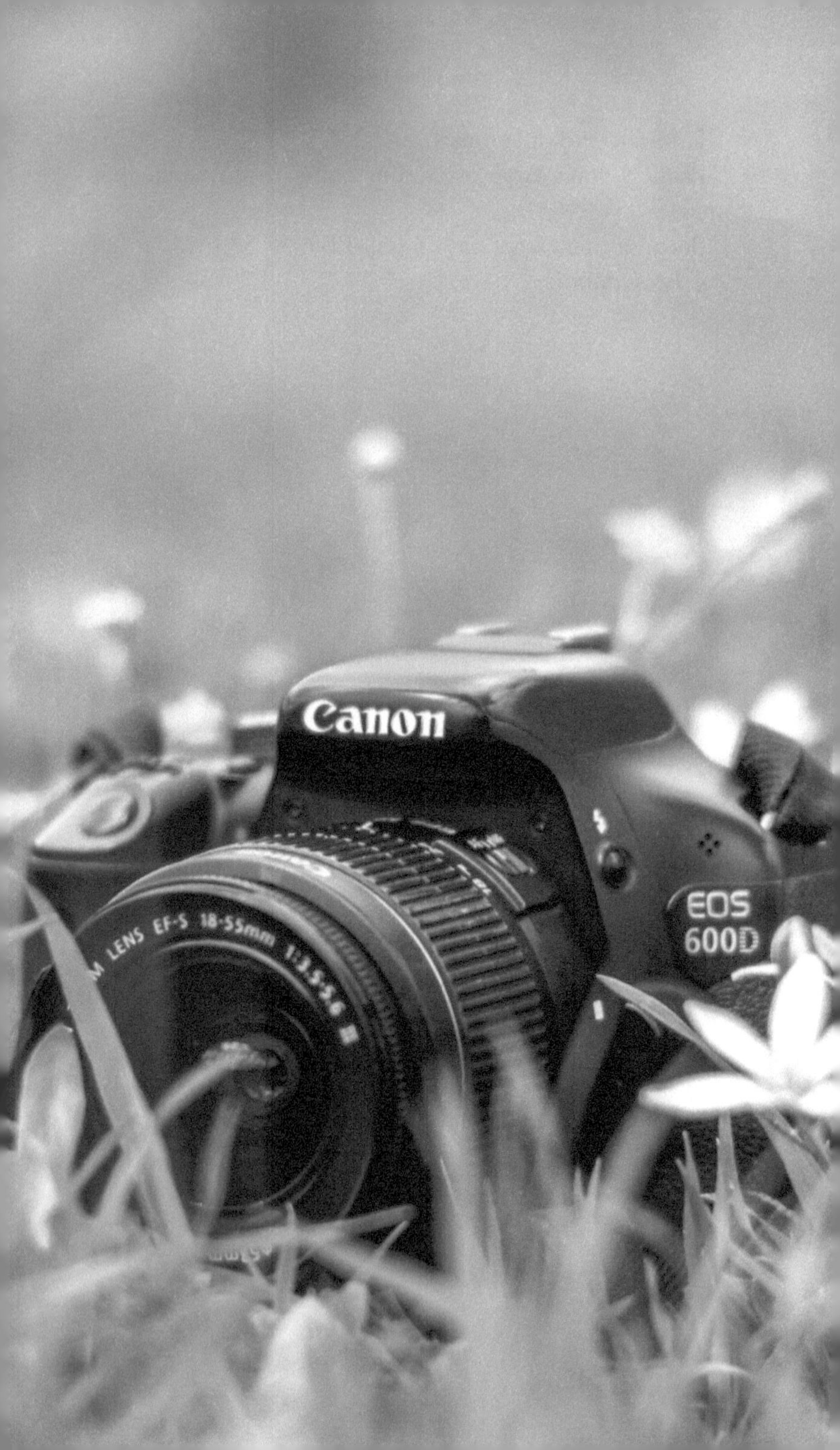
Canon
EOS
600D
LENS EF-S 18-55mm 1:3.5-5.6

Chapter Twenty

IVY

"I'm surprised I was able to drag you out today." I give Gemma a hug before sitting across from her in the booth.

"I should say the same about you."

"Me? Why?"

"You've been so busy watching Willow lately. Do I have to have a conversation with my brother about how hard he's working you?"

I school my face, not showing her what those words mean.

"It's fine. I'm glad I can help since he's been so busy at the bar."

"It's more than that." Our waitress stops by, dropping off a pitcher of mimosas and two glasses.

"Thanks for ordering." I fill up two glasses and gulp down half of mine.

"I knew we'd need it." She sips on hers. "What were we talking about?"

"You and that man of yours."

Gemma gives me a look. "More like my brother. He's been way too happy lately."

"Why is that a bad thing?"

"Oh my God. Do you know something?" Gemma asks.

"What? No. He barely says more than two words to me when he comes home after work."

I am the worst person. Lying to my closest friend in the world.

"Is he dating someone? Is that it?"

I shake my head, taking another big gulp of the fruity drink. I'm going to need a lot more of these if I'm going to make it through this breakfast with Gemma.

"Like I said, he doesn't tell me these things."

Gemma waves me off. "No. He probably wouldn't. You're just my best friend to him."

"I mean a little bit more than that." Her words hurt, even though I know she didn't mean them that way.

"I only mean that Mason doesn't see you as anything more than Willow's nanny and my friend. It's okay. It's not like you're dating him."

"No, that'd be crazy." My laugh is awkward.

"You two are so different. That's just insane."

I don't think we're that different. We actually go together pretty well.

Why am I arguing with her in my head? It's not like this thing with Mason is going to be permanent. I have a month left.

If I'm not spending my time with Willow, I'm sneaking away to meet Mason or out taking photographs.

As much as I love Gemma, even our time together has become less frequent because of her new guy.

"Speaking of people we're dating…" My face is hot. I need to move the conversation away from Mason and who he's not dating before I give us away. "How's Blake?"

"I'm so happy he's back."

"Mrs. Reynolds and Mrs. Phillips were all too happy to bring him their pies."

Gemma laughs, loud and bright. The conversation about her brother seems officially forgotten.

Good. Because I don't want to hear how she thinks Mason sees me. Even if it's the furthest thing from the truth.

"I don't know if he's ready for small-town life. He's going to have to learn to say no to them."

"I think he secretly loves it—being the center of attention."

"One of the perks of a small town." Our waitress comes back with our meals and sets them down. "I guess another perk. They know your order without even ordering."

"You won't get this in Seattle."

"Stop it." I cut off a bite of my banana pancake and eat it, chewing more thoroughly than I normally would. Once again, Gemma is steering the conversation where I don't want it to go.

"Are you ready for the big move?"

"I don't want to talk about it."

"It's all you've been talking about. It's finally here."

And now that it is, I'm having a hard time with it.

"Is it okay to feel weird about leaving?" I voice the small question. Not that Gemma needs to know the why of it all. But if I can't talk about these feelings with her, I might explode.

"Are you having second thoughts?"

"No, nothing like that." Her sole focus is on me. It's one of the reasons I love her. Whenever I need her, she is always there.

It makes the guilt of sneaking around with her brother behind her back press that much more on my mind.

"You've lived in Dixon your entire life. I'd be worried if you weren't nervous."

"It's a big change."

"Ivy." Gemma drops her fork and takes my hand in hers. "I've seen your work. You are an incredible photographer. The best I've seen."

"You have to say that. You're my best friend."

She shakes her head. "No, I don't. The work you show me? You're better than half those people out there. That's why I know this is an opportunity that you can't pass up."

Gemma's words warm me from the inside out. It's just what I need to hear. "Thanks, Gem."

"I'll remind you of it any time you need me to. The Layne Gallery is lucky to have you."

"And I'm lucky to have you."

"I'm not going anywhere. I know it'll be hard to get out to Seattle, but you're not getting rid of me anytime soon."

I laugh, because I know it's the truth. Gemma is my family. "Hopefully my apartment will be big enough for you to come visit."

"Hey, I'm a great bed partner if I need to be."

I waggle my eyebrows. "I'm sure Blake would agree with that."

"Stop it." Her face flushes. I love that I can still embarrass her like this, even though she's so far gone on Blake it's not even funny.

Just like I am with her brother.

Damn it.

No matter what I tell Gemma, leaving in a few weeks is going to be one of the hardest things I ever do. Because I have fallen so hard for Mason, I don't know what to do with myself.

It's pointless to lie at this point, even though I can't tell the truth to Gemma. I'm still leaving.

Leaving her, Mason, and Willow behind.

I don't know if my heart can withstand the loss.

Chapter Twenty-One

"Willow. Time to wake up, Pipsqueak."

Daisy jumps on her bed, giving her cheek a big lick.

She burrows farther under her blankets.

"C'mon, sweetheart. Ivy will be here soon."

Sad brown eyes peer up at me.

"My throat hurts, Daddy."

"Still?" I press a hand to her forehead.

Willow looks exhausted as I pull the covers back. Her cheeks are pink and her eyes are tired. It's a rare occurrence that I'm the one waking her up.

Her head is warm, but not burning up. At first I thought she caught the same bug I had. Except I was feeling better within forty-eight hours.

Almost five days later and she's still not feeling good.

"Can you stick your tongue out for me?" She opens her mouth, but not by much. It's red and irritated, with white spots.

Shit. This probably isn't good.

"Will you stay home with me?"

"Of course, Pipsqueak. Why don't you try and eat some breakfast, okay?"

She nods and I lift her easily into my arms. As she burrows into my neck, I pull out my phone, ready to text Ivy.

Except she's standing in my living room.

"Shit."

"Good morning to you too." Her eyes are playful as she takes me in.

Fuck. It's only been a few days since I last saw her. She's not wearing any makeup today, but she looks as beautiful as always.

Ivy stepped up for me. I've never had anyone to take care of me when I've been sick before. Sure, my family has helped with Willow, but I've always taken care of myself.

God. This woman. I'm in way too deep with her.

"Hi, Ivy." Willow sounds even worse than she looks as she picks her head up to see the woman who is consuming all of my thoughts.

"Are you still not feeling well, sweetheart?" Ivy tucks a loose strand of hair behind her ear.

"No." Her voice is wobbly.

"C'mere." Ivy takes her from me and heads into the living room.

It does funny things to my insides to see the two of them together. Turns out I'm not the only one falling for Ivy. Willow might love her even more than I do.

Shit.

Love?

Am I in love with Ivy? I can't be. This thing between us was supposed to be for the summer only.

I shake the thoughts from my head. I need to focus on Willow.

"What's wrong?" Ivy asks, tucking a blanket around her as Daisy lies next to her.

"My throat still hurts."

"Do you think ice cream will help?"

"Dunno," Willow says on a sigh. "Can we watch a show?"

"Sure."

Ivy turns on one of Willow's bright and sparkly rainbow episodes that usually make me crazy.

Today, it's a good distraction as I pull my phone out of my pocket and dial Willow's doctor.

"Mason. How are things?" Dr. Manning answers on the third ring.

One of the perks of a small town—being able to pick up the phone to call Willow's doctor and actually get to talk to him.

"Well, Willow's throat is hurting again."

"Does she have any white spots?" Dr. Manning asks.

"She does."

"I know we've discussed this, Mason, but I think it's time we get her in to get her tonsils removed."

"You think that's the best course of action?" I scrub a hand down my face. Willow is curled into Ivy's side, sleepy eyes on the TV. Ivy's running a hand through her hair.

"I do. We can do it now, or she can keep having this issue for a few months. Being that it's summer, she wouldn't miss any school if we remove them now."

"How soon can you get her in?" The last thing I want is Willow to be in any kind of pain.

"I have an opening first thing Monday morning if you want."

"And you really don't think there's any point in waiting?"

"If it were my daughter, I wouldn't. You don't want her to be in any more pain, and it will only get worse."

"Okay."

"It's a simple procedure, Mason. In and out," he reassures, "and Willow won't have to spend the night at the hospital. I'll get in touch with Ilene and have her get you on the books. She'll call you to get more information, but lots of fluids and rest for Willow until then. Children's Tylenol should help with any pain."

"You got it, doc. Thanks."

Hanging up the phone, I look over at the couch and Ivy's eyes are on me. I nod my head toward the kitchen, telling her to follow me.

"I'll be right back," Ivy tells Willow, tucking a pillow under her head. Willow yawns, snuggling in closer to Daisy as a burst of rainbows floods the TV screen.

"Everything okay?" Her voice is full of concern.

"The doctor wants to schedule her to get her tonsils out."

Ivy rests a hand on my forearm, giving it a squeeze. "You said this was a possibility."

I rub my hand over the back of my neck. "I know. But it doesn't make it easier to hear."

"Did they say when?"

"Monday."

Ivy peeks behind her—Willow is now fast asleep on the couch—and wraps me in a hug. I sink into her hold.

It's a simple hug, but something I need right now more than I ever imagined. This woman has woven her way into my life in a way I never knew I needed. It's always been just me and Willow.

And I was fine with that.

Not anymore.

I need Ivy more than I ever thought possible.

"It's going to be fine, Mason. Willow is a strong little girl, and you'll be there for her. And me. And the rest of the Winchester clan. She'll be well taken care of."

"Will you come with me?" I whisper into her ear.

"What?" Ivy pulls back.

Resting my forehead against hers, I gaze down into her blue eyes.

"I need you there with me."

"What about the rest of your family?"

"I'll tell them to stay home."

Ivy laughs. "And you think that will work?"

"I'll convince them. I want you there, Ivy. Willow will too."

I need Ivy by my side more than anyone else.

"Then I'll be there."

Now if only I could figure out a way to get her to stay by my side.

Permanently.

Chapter Twenty-Two

MASON

"When I invited you over tonight, I didn't think you'd actually come," Peter says by way of greeting.

"Nice to see you too, bro." I ruffle his hair as I walk into his cabin.

"You made it," Nash says, walking out of the kitchen with a bucket of beers.

"You make it sound like you haven't seen me in years. I saw you at the bar this morning."

Grabbing a beer, I sit on the couch opposite Logan. Its layout is identical to Gramps's house, except no upstairs. The kitchen and living room are in the center of the house with a bedroom and bathroom on each side. I know Logan likes it because he has his own space away from my brother and Nash.

Logan pins me with a look, sipping from his own drink. "But when have we seen you outside of the bar lately?"

"I'm sorry the single dad life doesn't work for your busy schedule."

"Yet, we've never had trouble getting you to come over

"

for guys' night before." Peter drops onto the loveseat with Nash.

Sometimes I really hate how observant family can be. Before, it used to be if I wasn't at the bar, I'd be at home with Willow.

I grab a piece of popcorn off the table and chuck it at Peter. "Maybe if you weren't so damn busy with your music festival, I'd have some time away from the bar."

"Hey! Blame Nash!"

"Why me?" Nash throws his hands up in defense. "I told you that you didn't have to help."

"If I wasn't helping, I'd never get to see you anymore." Peter drops down into his lap. "You wouldn't want that, would you?"

I'd be grossed out by their level of affection, but Peter was a moody bastard until Nash came back into his life.

"Willow wanted to have a girls' night with Gemma and Ivy before she gets her tonsils out on Monday."

"Shit. She has to have it done?" Logan asks.

"She does. She's scared of hospitals."

"Fuck," Logan mutters. "Is it because of me?"

I nod. I don't want to lie to him, but ever since Logan came home, she's been scared of them because he's been in and out of them for surgeries to repair his leg.

"I can talk to her if you need me to," Logan says. "Hand me a beer."

"She'll be okay. That's why she wanted Ivy and Gemma over tonight."

"Anything going on with you two?" Peter asks. He eyes me like he knows something.

What might he know? I have no idea. I've been careful, never wanting to mention Ivy's name for fear of someone picking up on what's going on between the two of us.

"She's Willow's nanny."

"So?" Nash asks.

I wave a finger between the two of them. "Do you two share the same brain now?"

"We've all been thinking it," Logan agrees, taking a long pull on his beer.

"I don't know where you fuckers think I'd have time to have a girlfriend. I'm either at the bar or with Willow."

"But you could date someone," Peter says. "Just not Ivy."

"I'm not dating Ivy."

"Good," Logan agrees. "There was a huge thing in high school because one of Gemma's friends liked me before I left for college and spread a bunch of rumors then ended up sleeping with Gemma's boyfriend."

Jesus. Now I feel like a shitty brother because Logan knew about this and I didn't.

"Nothing is going on."

The lie tastes like lead coming out of my mouth.

Ivy deserves better than that. She's not nothing. She's become the air I need to breathe. I have no idea how we're supposed to make this thing between the two of us work.

I want to. I really do.

But she's leaving in a few weeks. I can't do long distance. Hell, Willow can't do long distance. My life is here in Dixon. I can't pick up and travel at the drop of a hat. It's a twelve-plus hour drive to Seattle from here.

"Why aren't you bugging Logan about this?"

Logan gives me a deadpan stare. "I can barely walk without needing someone's help. You think I'm going to be able to go out on a date?"

"What's that girlfriend's name you had in Denver? Why isn't she here?"

"Because we broke up. Way to be a dick, Mason. Kick a man while he's down."

"Then don't bring up my love life."

Peter scoffs. "You never want to talk about your love life."

"When was the last time I had one?"

"I don't even think you had a girlfriend when I spent my summers here," Nash confirms. "You've never been a one-woman kind of guy."

"And you say I'm being the dick. I've never been the playboy you're making me out to be either. So sue me if I don't have time to focus on women."

All three of them are looking at me. I hate being the center of attention. Especially when this is the topic of discussion.

"Can we watch the game that I came over here to watch?"

"Someone really doesn't like us talking about him." Logan laughs. "It's what you get for being a dick and bringing up Audrey."

I flip him off. "Hey, at least you're up and hanging out. I've missed you, bro."

"Feels good." Logan gives me an easy smile.

It feels really good to be sitting here and having a few beers with my brothers. With Logan's leg causing so many issues, I was worried I'd never get something like this with him again.

But with him firmly on the road to recovery, my fears are somewhat assuaged. While I may not have let Logan down like I think I did, I know Gemma is going to be pissed if she finds out about me and Ivy.

There's not much I need in this world to be happy.

Willow. My family. Hell, even my job lets me work with family.

I wouldn't want it any other way.

Except Ivy. I can't figure out how I get to keep her in

my life. It's like a speeding train is racing down the track to her leaving, and it's only going to end in a terrible crash.

With the two of us at the center. If only there was another way. Another track we could get on so it doesn't end with heartbreak.

If only…

Canon
EOS
600D
M LENS EF-S 18-55mm 1:3.5-5.6 III

Chapter Twenty-Three

Of all days to be late. My alarm didn't go off this morning, and now I'm rushing to the medical center to sit with Mason during Willow's procedure.

Poor thing was scared to pieces last night, and I hated leaving her. The entire Winchester family was with her, so it's not like she needed me. But when she asked for me to come to the hospital, sticking out that pouty lip she's mastered, I couldn't say no.

I love that kid something fierce, and it's going to hurt like hell when I leave in a few weeks.

My phone rings as I pull a sweatshirt over my head. It's a Seattle number. One I don't recognize.

"Hello?" I answer, shoving my feet into my shoes and heading out the door.

"Is this Ivy Connors?" a voice comes over the line.

"It is."

"Hi. This is Janet from the Layne Gallery."

My ears perk up at the name of my new employer. "Oh. Hi."

"I know this might seem sudden, but we were wondering if you could start next week."

"Next week? I thought I wasn't set to start until the beginning of September."

It's the beginning of August. I still have a few more weeks here in Dixon before I'm supposed to move.

"We have a brand-new exhibit opening, and I figure what better way to start off than working an opening."

Leaning against my front door, I take a deep breath. This really isn't what I needed to be dealing with right now. My focus needs to be on Willow and being there for her.

"Can I look at my schedule and get back to you?"

"Sure, sure. This is a great opportunity, and I would hate for you to miss out."

"Thanks, Janet. I'll let you know tomorrow if that works?"

"Perfect. Thanks, Ivy." She hangs up without another word.

I want to shout yes with every fiber of my being. This is exactly why I took this job in Seattle. The Layne Gallery is an up-and-coming gallery that's known to bring in the big art collectors. Having a place like this to start my career? I'd be stupid to turn down such an incredible opportunity.

For as long as I can remember, moving out of Dixon has been my dream. To put this small town in my rearview mirror and not look back.

So why am I having second thoughts now?

"Mason? Where is everyone?"

Mason is the only one in the hospital waiting room by the time I get there.

He unfurls himself from the plastic chair. There's nothing soothing or calming about the small room he's in. Bright, overhead lights are harsh as paintings of flowers try to calm those waiting here for news on loved ones.

"I told them not to come."

"And they listened?" I look around, making sure we're alone, before pulling Mason into my arms.

"I'm as surprised as you."

"Did they already take Willow back?"

He nods against me.

"I'm sorry I wasn't here on time."

Mason squeezes me closer to him. "They took her back earlier than planned, so she'll be out soon."

"You're doing okay?" I pull back, rubbing at the wrinkles in his forehead.

"I'll be better once she's done. Who knew tonsils would wreak this much havoc on someone?"

I smile, pulling Mason down into the chairs.

"For Willow or you?"

"Me. You know Willow will be happy getting to eat popsicles all day."

Mason's hand comes down on my leg. His warmth spreads through me. I wrap my arms around his bicep.

"And getting all the attention? She's a lucky little girl."

"That she is," Mason whispers into my hair, dropping a kiss there.

A pang cuts through my chest, as the call from earlier weighs heavy on my mind.

This summer was supposed to be about having fun and enjoying what time I had left before moving to Seattle.

I never thought that the crush I had on Mason Winchester would turn into this. Into something more.

My dreams were always bigger than this town. With a tumultuous childhood here, I didn't plan on finding someone in Dixon.

Sure, a few fun flings here and there, but nothing serious. I didn't want it. I want wings, not roots.

Now? Now everything is all twisted up in my head. The biggest opportunity is at my fingertips. In Seattle.

More than twelve hours away.

Sitting here with Mason is messing with my head.

He was supposed to be a fling.

He was *supposed to be* temporary.

Now, I can't tell what I want him to be.

"Mr. Winchester?" The doctor comes into the waiting room. Mason flies up out of my hold.

"Is she out of surgery?"

He nods, a smile on his face. "Everything went beautifully. The nurses are getting her settled in her room, and they'll be up to take you there in a few minutes."

"Thanks, doc." Mason shakes his hand before the doctor heads back between the swinging doors.

Mason bends over, blowing out a huge breath.

"See? Everything was fine." I rub a hand over his back, trying to soothe away his lingering worries.

"Thank God." Standing to his full height, Mason brings me flush with his body. I'm aware of every place we're touching.

I don't think. I act. Pressing up onto my tiptoes, I take his lips in a warm kiss. He sinks into my hold. My veins are buzzing as he holds me to him.

There's nothing heated about this kiss. But it still sets my entire body on fire. Because this man is what I've always wanted.

"What the hell?" Gemma's voice interrupts us.

"Oh, shit," Mason whispers, taking a step back from me.

Spinning on my heel, I see Gemma standing in the doorway of the waiting room with a stuffed animal in her hand.

"What are you doing here?" I blurt out.

"Me? I should ask you the same thing?"

Gemma is horrified.

"I…" I glance back at Mason, not knowing what to say or do.

The one rule we had about this thing between us is that Gemma wouldn't find out.

And we just blew it wide open.

The nurse comes into the waiting room. "Mr. Winchester. If you'd like, you can see Willow now."

Mason looks between the three of us, not knowing what to do.

"Go see Willow." Squeezing his arm, I try to send him with the nurse.

His eyes dip down to meet mine. Worry is written across his face.

"I don't want to leave you to deal with this," he whispers, but not soft enough.

"Maybe if one of you told me what was going on…"

I turn back to Gemma. I don't think I've ever seen her so mad before. Steam is practically shooting out of her ears.

"Give Willow this. I guess I don't need to see her since Ivy is here." She shoves the stuffed animal at Mason and leaves.

As much as I want to be here for Mason, I can't right now. I don't know what is spinning through Gemma's mind, and I don't want her to leave.

"Go be with your daughter. She needs you more than I do." I give him a sad smile.

"Will you be okay?" He nods at the door Gemma just left through.

"We'll be fine." I hope. "Just go."

Mason nods once before following the nurse. I run out the door after my oldest friend. I can't let her leave without talking to her.

"Gemma! Wait up!" She's in the parking lot by the time I find her. When she turns to face me, tears sting her eyes.

"Were you ever going to tell me? Just having a laugh when I said to have a summer fling and you found the first guy you could?"

"Gemma. It's not like that."

She scoffs. "It certainly feels like that. You lied to me, Ivy."

I wince at her words. I know I lied. But it's not like I wanted to. Gemma is reacting exactly how I thought she would if she found out about us.

"We didn't want to tell you because I knew you'd be upset."

"No shit. You lied to me and then I had to find out when my niece is in the hospital! You should have told me, Ivy."

"And have you hate me because I've been sleeping with your brother?"

Her hands fly to her ears. "I don't want to hear that! You know how bad it got with Avery," she hisses. "You were the only person that was there for me."

"What, so you really think I'm going to cut you out of my life if your brother dumps me?"

This time, Gemma just looks sad. "Yes. This is a small town, Ivy. It's not like you wouldn't bump into each other all the time. I don't want to be a painful reminder of what you don't have."

"It's not like I'm sticking around."

Gemma rears back like I slapped her. "That's right. You're too good for Dixon."

"You know that's not what I meant." I scrub a hand down my face. This is getting us nowhere.

"You're just fooling around then with my brother and saying 'see ya' at the end of the summer?"

"Gemma…"

"Am I wrong, Ivy? You're leaving in a few weeks. You said so yourself."

I hate that she's right. I'll never tell her that in this moment, but she is. This thing with Mason was never supposed to be serious. Just a way for the two of us to blow off steam this summer. A fling. Feelings weren't supposed to get involved. It makes it messy.

Telling family and friends—especially this friend— makes it even messier.

We wanted good, clean fun.

Now it's anything but fun.

I thought we had a few more weeks together. Now, it's done. Over. Over before we really had a chance to get started.

"No. I'm still going to Seattle."

Gemma shakes her head at me. In all the time I've known her, I've never seen her this upset with me. Sure, we had the occasional stupid fight over silly things in high school. But the anger coming off her now is something I've never felt.

"So you're leaving and that's that."

The sadness in her voice hits me square in the chest. Now I don't know if she's mad at me for leaving or for the whole thing with Mason.

"Can we talk about this when you're not upset?" I plead. Standing in the middle of the hospital parking lot isn't the best place for this.

"Blake and I are leaving for LA tomorrow and we'll be back next week." She tucks a stray lock of hair behind her ear.

Next week. When I'll be in Seattle starting my new job.

I pull Gemma into a hug. "Go be with Willow. Don't be mad at Mason. I'll see you when I see you."

"Fine."

She stalks off into the hospital without a look back.

Fuck.

I stab a hand through my hair and head to my car. My phone buzzes in my pocket.

MASON

Are you okay?

I punch out a response.

I'll be fine. Tell Willow I'm thinking of her

I doubt he'll believe me. But what else is there to say?

I fell in love with my best friend's brother when it was supposed to be a fling and ended up hurting my best friend.

And breaking my own heart in the process.

Maybe it is just better if I leave town now.

Opening my phone, I dial the last number in my recent calls list. It goes straight to voicemail. I guess it's better this way as tears start to fill my eyes.

"Hi, Janet. It's Ivy Connors. I wanted to let you know there won't be any issues with starting next week. Looking forward to it."

I end the call and toss my phone into the front seat. Turning on my car, I leave the hospital.

And put the three people I love most in my rearview mirror.

Chapter Twenty-Four

MASON

"Daddy, do we have to go to dinner tonight?"

"What? Why wouldn't you want to go to family dinner?"

Willow burrows farther into the couch. With summer coming to an end, she'd usually be playing outside with her friends from sunup to sundown. Instead, she's been moping around the house.

"My throat still hurts."

I drop down onto the coffee table, taking in my sweet daughter. Her eyes are sad. Everything about her face is sad right now. This is not the bright and happy Willow that she normally is.

I feel her head. No fever. "You don't feel warm."

She sighs. "It's my throat. Not my head."

The doctor cleared her at her last appointment. I'm guessing it has to do with a certain person who is no longer in town.

"Maybe seeing everyone will make you feel better, Pipsqueak."

Willow shrugs a shoulder.

"How about this." I scoop her into my arms. "If you don't feel better after dinner, we'll leave and make sundaes. How does that sound?"

That perks her up. "Okay, Daddy."

Dropping a kiss on her head, I set her down on her feet. "Go grab your shoes and we'll head out."

Willow runs off.

It's been like this ever since Ivy left.

One minute she was here, the next she was gone. I don't know what happened with her and Gemma at the hospital. I had other things to worry about. Like Willow.

Gemma barely said two words to me at the hospital. I couldn't even talk to her after because she's been in LA with Blake.

She'll be at dinner tonight. And that's part of the reason I want to go. Something happened to send Ivy running. She didn't just leave me. She left Willow.

Logically, I know she was going to leave at the end of the summer. But we still had time together. Ever since she left, Willow and I have been struggling. It's like she took everything good with her.

So much for being a summer fling.

I gave Ivy my heart and she took it with her.

"Ready, Daddy!" Willow comes around the corner in a pair of unicorn rain boots. There hasn't been a rainy day since that big storm blew through.

Fuck. Once again I'm thinking about Ivy.

Will I ever stop thinking about her?

"Let's go, Willow." Grabbing my keys, we head out. Instead of Willow chattering my ears off, she's quiet.

I hate it. I fucking hate it.

"What are you doing at camp tomorrow?" I ask, trying to draw anything out of her.

"I dunno. I think we're tie-dyeing tomorrow."

"That'll be fun. Are you making T-shirts?"

"I think so. My counselor was wearing one today and it was really cool."

"Oh yeah?" I flit my gaze back to her before turning it back to the road. That gets her going. Willow starts telling me about the counselors at camp and the new friends she's made. It puts a smile on my face for the first time since Ivy left.

"And we even get to do archery! I'm going to be so good, Daddy!"

"You're going to kick everyone's ass," I tell her, pulling into Gramps's driveway.

"I don't think I'm allowed to say that."

I laugh. "Maybe not, but you will."

"Maybe Uncle Blake should come to camp and learn. He's not very good."

"Next time you stay with Aunt Gemma, you can show him your skills."

Willow snickers as she unbuckles her seatbelt as soon as the truck is in park. Gramps is outside waiting for us.

"Gramps!"

"How's my favorite girl?"

Willow starts rattling off the same stories to my grandpa. I clap him on the shoulder as I head inside. Almost everyone is already gathered in the living room.

"No Logan tonight?"

"He wasn't feeling up to it." Nash hands me a beer.

"Nothing wrong post-surgery?" I don't know when the worry will stop for Logan. Maybe once he's finally in the clear.

"Everything looked good. He was just tired."

Gemma comes in from the kitchen. When her eyes find me, they turn hard.

"Mason."

Fine. If that's how she wants to play it.

"Gemma."

"Is this how you two are going to be all night?" Peter asks, shaking his head.

"We're being perfectly civil," Gemma says, walking back into the kitchen.

"What did I miss?" Nash is looking around.

"Gemma's mad that Ivy and Mason were sleeping together," Peter tells him.

"And I'm guessing she didn't know?" Nash asks.

"It's not like it was any of her business," I bite out. I hate being the topic of conversation. Especially over something that is still so raw.

Because that's exactly what this feels like. It's raw. Like a big, festering, open wound that won't close. One minute I'll feel okay. And the next I'll feel bad for feeling okay.

Because we were temporary, right? Ivy clearly didn't see me as anything worth sticking around for, so why should I stress?

"Soooo, you don't want to talk about it?" Nash asks. Peter leans over, whispering in his ear. "We're going to go check on dinner."

"Real subtle, guys."

"Be thankful they're not asking you questions." Layla elbows me in the side.

I know how much she hated being on the receiving end of all the attention after her divorce. I hate it even more than she does.

I like my privacy. As much as I love my family, it can be overbearing at times.

I don't want to sit and rehash everything that went wrong.

"You're not going to ask me any questions?" I sip on my beer.

Layla shakes her head. "Nope. Because I hated it, so I'm not going to make you suffer."

"I knew you were my favorite."

"I thought I was your favorite!" Willow bounces up to me, running into the house before Gramps.

"Of course you're my favorite, Pipsqueak. You'll always be my favorite."

Willow leaps into my arms. "You're my favorite too, Daddy." She drops a kiss on my cheek and wiggles out of my hold. "I'm hungry. When are we going to eat?"

"Right now!" Gemma comes out of the kitchen, looking a bit friendly. "Want to sit next to me, Willow?"

She nods and follows her over to the table. Better her sitting next to Gemma than me.

Now that I'm here, the anger is starting to come in.

I don't know what happened. That's the worst part. Ivy left with a quick text that her job started sooner than she anticipated and that was it. She wouldn't answer any of my calls or texts.

Who does that?

"How's work going?" Nash asks Layla.

"It looks like I'm not going to get the bigger space across the street."

"Why not?" Nash passes the bowl of green pepper steak to me.

"Because of Brad."

"Who's that?" Blake asks.

"I'll tell you later," Gemma whispers.

"Someone who lives to make my life a living hell." Layla stabs a pepper onto her fork and shoves it into her mouth.

"How was camp, Willow?" Gemma asks her, changing the subject.

She goes off onto another tangent about camp.

"What's with you tonight?" Peter nudges me.

"I'm fine." I stab my own piece of steak and pop it in my mouth.

"You've been off all week," Nash agrees.

"Can you please drop it?"

"Hey, we've got a big few weeks coming up. I need you on your A game."

"Have I not been on it all week?" I drop my fork, turning to look at both of them.

"I mean, crabbier than usual, but fine," Peter says.

"Aunt Gemma, do you know why Ivy left?" Willow asks, shifting my attention once again. I love her innocence. She has no idea why Ivy left.

"Ivy left?" Gemma asks, turning to face me.

"Willow, why don't you go play video games upstairs?" I tell her. I want to know Gemma's answer.

Because she has to know something.

"I thought I wasn't allowed any screen time after dinner?"

"Tonight's an exception." I smile at her from across the table.

"Yes!" She throws her fist up in the air.

I wait until I hear the ding of the machine through the thin walls before facing Gemma. She's got a fighting look on her face.

"Same question, Gem. Do you know why Ivy left?" I don't hide the bitterness from my voice.

"Throwing it back to you. Ivy left?"

"Don't act like you don't know."

Everyone's eyes are ping-ponging back and forth between the two of us.

"I got home yesterday from LA. I called her and she didn't pick up."

"Wait, really?"

Gemma nods. "I texted with her a few times, but nothing that was important."

"So you didn't know she was leaving?"

"Mason." Gemma's voice is soft, like she's trying to coddle me. "She was always going to leave."

"It doesn't make it any easier," I mumble.

"She said it was a summer fling."

"It wasn't for me."

"Oh, holy shit," Nash whispers next to me. "You love her."

"You love her?" Gemma gasps.

"Of course I fucking love her, okay?" My outburst stuns everyone into silence. "I wouldn't be acting like this if I didn't love her."

"What?"

"Holy shit."

"This is better than my show." Everyone's talking over each other, but Blake's words ease the growing tension in the room.

"Blake." Gemma slaps him on the chest and turns back to me. "You really love her?"

"As much as I don't want to, yeah. And she's gone. Willow and I are miserable without her."

"Oh, Mason." Gemma pops out of her chair and walks over to me. "I'm so sorry. This is all my fault."

I scrub a hand down my face. "It's not. Like you said, she was always going to leave. She was just looking for a reason."

"So? Bring her back."

"It's not that easy, Gem. I wish it were. She never wanted Dixon."

Never wanted me.

And that's something that I'm going to have to come to terms with. Because I can't be this sad sack for the rest of my life. I have to get my shit together for my daughter. Show her that we'll both be okay without Ivy.

No matter how much I want to be the reason she stayed, she's gone.

And not coming back.

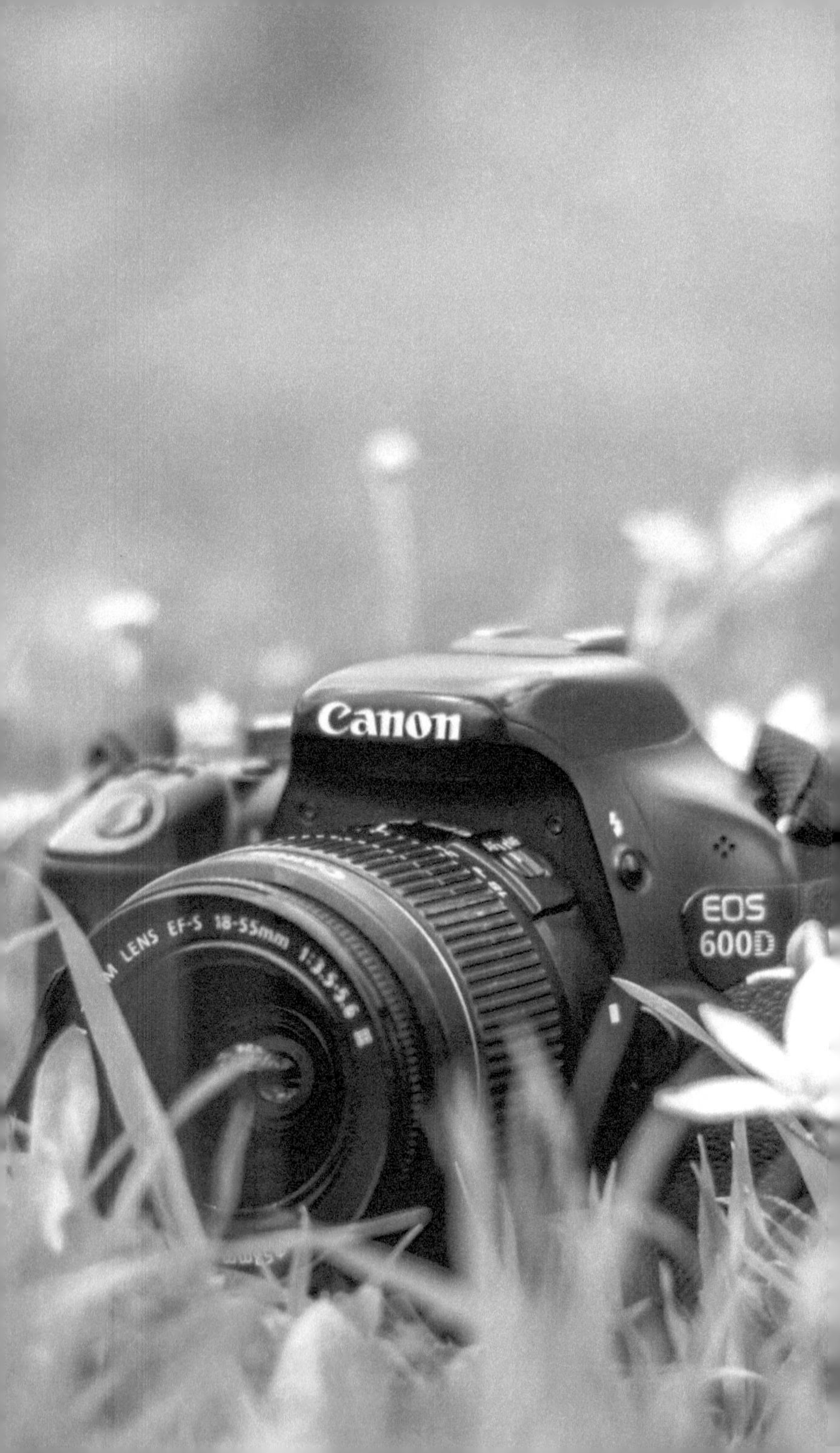
Canon
EOS
600D
LENS EF-S 18-55mm 1:3.5-5.6

Chapter Twenty-Five

IVY

A blaring horn startles me awake. It's something I'm still not used to. The constant noise. No matter what time of day, there's always something.

Sirens. People yelling. Horns.

Sighing, I get out of bed and pad out to the kitchen. The studio apartment I found is nothing special. It was the only place I could get on such short notice since my original apartment wasn't ready.

It doesn't bother me.

Because everywhere I look, I'm reminded of what this place isn't.

Too much noise.

Too many people.

Not enough open fields. Or the mountains I love.

It's not Dixon.

Popping a coffee pod in the machine, I watch the dark brew drip into my mug.

I should be happy. This art gallery position is everything I've ever wanted and worked for. Even though the

Layne Gallery is a small one, it has the potential to open up a lot of doors for me.

Gemma's face pops into my mind.

The hurt at me lying to her about sleeping with her brother. About telling her I wasn't staying in Dixon.

I was a coward. Instead of facing her—facing Mason—like an adult, I ran. It was too hard. I didn't want the yelling that I'd grown up with.

A clean break.

Except it's anything but clean.

Because I broke my own damn heart when I left town.

I should be out enjoying the city. Enjoying all that Seattle has to offer.

But I can't.

The pinging of the coffee machine pulls me out of my spinning thoughts. I add more cream than necessary, downing half the cup in two big swallows. I need it if I want to make it through the day.

With one of the new portrait exhibits opening tonight, it's going to be a long day, working to make sure everything is perfect.

This is why I started early—for this upcoming show.

Heading into the bathroom, I go through the motions of getting ready for the day. Hair. Makeup. A brand-new white silk blouse with a black pencil skirt I bought especially for the opening.

I'm hoping by looking my best, I'll feel my best.

Too nervous to eat, I dump the rest of the coffee into a travel mug and am out the door.

A wall of heat slams into me. I shrug out of my blazer. It's a sticky morning, so hot, you can see the heat hanging in the sky. Thankfully it's only a short walk to the gallery.

Even this early in the morning, the sidewalks are filled

with people. Skyscrapers kiss the sky on both sides of me. The Space Needle stands tall in the distance.

It's something I still can't quite get used to. This view.

Having had mountains my entire life, it still blows me away.

Not paying attention to where I'm walking, it happens in slow motion.

I run smack into someone.

"Watch it!" he shouts. The lid pops off my mug, spilling the last dregs of coffee down my blouse. My very white blouse.

"Fuck."

Tears sting my eyes. With everything else going on, this is the last thing I need to deal with.

"Fuck."

Spinning on my heel, I head back to my apartment.

So much for feeling good about today.

EVERYTHING about this night is perfect. The lights are dim, with small lights spotlighting the works of art hanging on the walls. Champagne is flowing. It's packed to the brim with people.

After a disaster of a morning, I was able to settle down and focus on work, and now I'm schmoozing all the biggest art collectors in the Seattle area.

A group of people move around the old industrial space turned art gallery. The crowd spreads out and reveals a familiar face.

"Gemma?" With a glass of champagne in hand, she walks over to me. Just seeing her makes a wave of homesickness slam into me. "What in the world are you doing here?"

She's tanner than she usually is—no doubt from her trip to LA. Gemma is as stunning as ever in a simple black dress.

"You ran out of town when I was gone. What else was I supposed to do?"

"But you were so mad at me."

She waves me off and pulls me into a hug. "And I was over it by the time I got home. You just didn't give me a chance to apologize."

"I can't believe you're here. Why are you here?" My voice comes out all watery.

No matter how much I try to convince myself I'm okay, I'm not. Not even close.

Gemma squeezes me even tighter. "Because I saw Mason."

This time, I can't help the tears that leak out of my eyes. "How are they?"

Because it's not just Mason I miss. I miss Willow and spending my days with her just as much.

Gemma pulls back, clasping my cheeks in her hands. "Honestly? Kind of terrible."

I grab her hand and pull her into an unoccupied corner of the gallery. People are still everywhere, and I don't want them to hear this conversation.

I cross my arms, almost like a shield for this conversation. "It's not like we could've been anything. This is where my life is."

"Are you happy here though?" Gemma quirks a brow at me.

"Does it matter? I've never wanted to live in Dixon."

"How many times have you told yourself that since you got here?"

At least once an hour. But I don't tell her that.

"Gemma. Running a gallery like this is what I've always wanted. To live in the city and travel."

She grabs my arms. "But are you happy?"

"I can be. I just need to get settled. It's a big change from Dixon."

Gemma shudders. "I'm pretty sure I saw three cop cars go by on my way here. And that was one block."

That gets a laugh out of me. "I don't know if I'll ever get used to all the sirens. And all the football fans. They are crazy here."

Gemma makes a disgusted face. "There's only one team as far as I'm concerned."

"Shh! I don't want you getting into a fight here."

"I'll take 'em. Mountain Lions are the only team anyone should cheer for."

"God, I've missed you." I wrap my arms around her.

"Come home." She squeezes me even tighter to her. "It's not Dixon without you."

"Ivy. There's an interested buyer on the *Summer Nights in Bloom* piece. Would you talk to them since you're familiar with it?" One of the other gallery attendants finds me.

I smile back at him. "Sure."

He smiles back at me. "Show us why we brought you here."

"How long are you here?" I ask Gemma. Seeing her is the first time I've felt settled since I got here.

"Until Sunday."

"Good. I'll come find you when I'm done." I give her a quick hug before heading over to the piece in question.

An older woman with a short, bright blue pixie cut is standing in front of my favorite photo in the new opening.

"Hi there."

She turns a beaming smile on me. Bright pink lipstick

paints her smile. Heavy gold earrings drag down her lobes. Necklaces too many to count adorn her chest.

"Hi, dear."

"You're interested in this piece?" I nod to the artwork in front of us.

It's a stunning picture. In the Canadian Rockies, flowers are in full color while the starry summer sky is bright behind them.

It's beautiful in its simplicity. I love it because it reminds me of home.

Home. The one place I never thought I wanted to be turned out to be the place I love most.

"I have to have it. Money is no object."

I stifle a smile. "Well, that's an easy sale."

"I know what I like."

"I didn't catch your name."

"Sasha."

I hold out my hand to her. "Ivy."

"It's nice to meet you."

"You too. Do you have other similar pieces?"

Sasha takes a swig of her champagne. "I do. I'm also looking at opening my own gallery."

"You are?"

She nods. "My husband and I are retiring. We want someone to source pieces for us, but also open our own place to share our love of art."

"Well, Seattle is a great place for that."

Sasha waves me off. "Oh no. I'm done with the city."

I have to choke back the laugh. I'm done with the city and I've only been here a few weeks. "How long have you lived here?"

"Too long. I want some fresh mountain air." Sasha looks back toward the photo hanging on the wall. "Something like this. A place I can explore."

"The mountains are great for that."

"You sound like you have experience."

"I'm from a small town near the Tetons."

Sasha's eyes light up. "I've always heard how beautiful that area is."

"Makes for great photos. The lighting. The flowers. And that fresh mountain air you were talking about."

"Are you a photographer yourself? Do you have any pieces up tonight?"

I shake my head. "Not tonight, no. But maybe someday."

Sasha pulls out a card and hands it to me. "I don't want to keep you. I know you're busy tonight, but how about we grab some coffee tomorrow? I'd love to keep talking to you. Maybe see some of your work."

"Really?" I take the card in my hand, holding it like a lifeline. The first person I've met in the city who actually seems to care.

"Call me, Ivy."

After I hand her over to the accountant to get her payment information, Sasha leaves and Gemma is back at my side.

"Who was that?"

I don't know, but I have a feeling she might change my life.

Canon
EOS
600D
ZOOM LENS EF-S 18-55mm 1:3.5-5.6

Chapter Twenty-Six

IVY

"Ivy! I'm so happy you could meet me today." Sasha greets me with open arms, her jasmine perfume heavy in the coffee shop.

"I'm happy to."

After the gallery opening last night, I soaked up as much time with Gemma as I could. Even going a few weeks without her was too much.

A girl needs her best friend.

"Did you buy anything else last night?" I take the seat opposite her and set down my mug of coffee I ordered before coming over.

"No. I couldn't see anything else besides those mountains."

I smile. "They really are beautiful."

"So, you said last night you are a photographer?" she asks, sipping on her own coffee. Her eyes are glittering as the Seattle sound stretches out behind her. The small coffee shop on the water is just what I needed this morning.

"I am."

"Do you have anything I can see?"

"Sure."

Pulling out my phone, I find the album with all the photos I've taken recently and hand it over to her.

I study her as she flips through each photo. Her face gives nothing away.

This is always the hardest part when showing my work to others. What will they think?

Too basic?

Not enough character?

Not enough emotion?

"Ivy."

"Do you like them?"

I wait with bated breath.

"Like them? I love them. How are you not showing these in galleries already?"

"You think they're that good?"

"They're stunning. The way you capture the light in the mountains. It's even better than the piece I bought last night."

"Are you serious?"

The piece Sasha bought last night was shot by a world-renowned photographer. So to hear her say this really means something.

"What would you say to running a gallery?" She points to my phone. "Here. Wherever this is."

"What?" I'm stunned speechless.

"These photos need to be shown to the world."

"But in Dixon?"

"Is that where these were shot? I've never heard of it."

I shake the fog out of my brain and take another long drag of hot coffee. "I just started this job here. I can't leave."

Sasha leans forward, clasping her ringed fingers together. "Will you answer this question honestly for me?"

"Okay…" I'm nervous for whatever it might be.

"Do you like it here in Seattle?"

I blow out a breath. "It's been an adjustment."

"That's a no," Sasha says on a laugh.

"It's not a no!" I defend. But even I can hear that my words have no gusto in them.

"City living isn't for everyone."

"I've only been here for a little while. I can still adjust."

Sasha grabs my hand. "You're in your twenties, right? This should be the most exciting time of your life. Going out to bars. Meeting handsome men, or women if you're into them, and partying until dawn. You, my dear, look miserable."

Shit. "I thought I was doing a better job hiding it."

"What would make you happy?"

Mason and Willow pop into my mind. Being with them. Loving them. Starting a life with them.

Can I really have it all though?

"Whatever you just thought of, that makes you happy. Who is it?" Sasha has a knowing grin on her face.

"There was this guy and his daughter. He's my best friend's older brother and I ran out of town without looking back."

"They make you happy. But you were also happy last night at the gallery."

"I love art. It's what I want to do. Have a gallery. Travel to acquire new pieces. Bring art to people who love it."

"What if I could give that to you?"

"What?"

I couldn't have heard her right.

"All that. A gallery. Traveling. These photos you took in Dixon? I want more. We can do this together."

"Me? Running your gallery? I can't."

"Why not?"

"I just started this job, for one."

Sasha waves me off. "I know Janet. I'll buy another piece from her to soothe the sting."

I throw her question back to her. "Would you be happy living in Dixon? It's a tiny town."

"Honey, I'm old and I know what I want. I've done the big city. I told you, I want that mountain air."

"I can see you fitting in nicely in Dixon."

"Everything is what you make it, dear." Sasha extends a bangled wrist to me. "So, what do you say? Want to go into business with me?"

I clasp her warm hand in mine, butterflies dancing in my stomach.

"Holy shit. Are we really going to do this?"

Sasha is beaming. "You bet your ass we are. Now, I think this calls for a celebration worth more than coffee. How about some champagne?"

My smile matches hers. "Let's do it."

Because this woman who I've known for less than twenty-four hours is going to give me everything I want. A way back to Dixon, doing what I love, and hopefully back into the arms of the man I love.

My own blue-haired fairy godmother.

Chapter Twenty-Seven

MASON

"Are you going to be okay with Gramps tonight?" I set Mr. Dino down next to Willow on the couch. With heaps of coloring books around her, I know she'll be content. For the first time since Ivy left, she's finally doing better. I don't want to leave her, but I don't want to *not* be there for Nash on his big night.

Musicians Take Dixon.

Nash has been working hard on this for months. I want to be there to support him.

"I'll be fine." She ignores me, coloring the dinosaur. Ever since she got her new stuffed animal at the fair, it's all she's wanted to have around.

Gramps pats me on the back. "Willow will be okay. I've taken care of my fair share of kids."

I scrub a hand down my face. Ever since Ivy left, I've been a mess. Both of us. Willow's finally stopped crying that she's gone, but every morning I wake up with an ache in my chest, and I don't know if it'll ever go away.

At least now I'm not tiptoeing around my sister,

blaming her. Because Ivy did exactly what she said she was going to do.

She left.

"Sorry. I worry."

"You worry too much. Now go. Enjoy Peter and Nash's big night."

I give Gramps a quick hug and drop a kiss on Willow's head. "I love you, Willow."

"Love you, Daddy," she sighs.

Fuck. I hate how sad she's been since Ivy left.

Ivy didn't just leave me. She left Willow too.

That's the worst part. Willow loved her just as much as I did.

I guess we really were a summer fling to her.

Hopping into my truck, I head out of town. It's at the same place as the fair was.

Why does every fucking thing in this town remind me of Ivy?

I hate it. She didn't want to be here. She didn't want to stay with us. So I shouldn't be worried about her. I shouldn't be missing her.

But I am.

She left and ripped my heart out and took it with her.

I knew I never should've started anything with her.

And the worst part isn't me. It's seeing Willow so damn sad. I can handle most things. Seeing my daughter sad when I can't help? It's the worst feeling in the world knowing I can't do anything to make her feel better.

Bypassing all the cars turning into the parking lot, I head for the VIP area. One of the perks of being related to the organizers.

Not that Peter and Nash are married, but Nash is basically part of the family.

Grabbing my VIP badge, I follow the lines of people

heading into the makeshift stage. I see Gemma up ahead, pushing what looks to be Logan in his wheelchair.

Well, I'll be damned. I'm glad I came tonight if only for seeing my brother outside of the house or rehab center.

Peter and Nash are in their own world as people hustle around them.

"Holy shit. If all it took was a music festival to get our brother out, I would've suggested you throw one months ago."

I wrap an arm around Peter and Nash.

"I'm glad you could make it. You've been preoccupied lately," Nash tells me.

"No comment." I ruffle his hair, ignoring him.

I'm glad Nash is here. He and my brother are absolutely perfect for each other.

"Wait, does that mean something happened?" Peter asks.

"Like I said, no comment." I push between the two of them and follow after Gemma to the stage.

The last thing I want is another conversation about Ivy. Nothing's changed, so I don't know why they're asking.

Ivy's gone. End of story.

A band is already playing by the time I find my way to the wings of the main stage.

"Look what the cat dragged in. Or, I guess I should say, out." I slap Logan on the chest from behind. He looks up at me, a small smile on his face. It's something I haven't seen in a long time.

It's really fucking good to see.

"I couldn't miss this. It's basically the only thing they've been talking about all summer."

"You sure you don't want to move in with me and Willow?" I offered it when he first came home, but he didn't want to.

I think it's more to do with protecting Willow than anything. We've spared her the worst of Logan's injury. She loves her uncle too much to see the worst of it.

"Nah. I'm good. I'm hoping this next surgery will be the last."

"You and me both."

Gemma walks back up, sipping on a beer and handing Logan a water bottle.

"Mason. I didn't think you'd be here tonight."

"Why not?"

"She thought you'd be moping," Logan says.

I roll my eyes and steal her cup of beer and take my own sip. "I haven't been moping."

"Logan said you were."

I smack my brother in the head. "Really?"

"Hey. I'm injured. Don't hurt me."

"Your head is fine."

I can't believe my brother sold me out.

"I feel bad though. I feel like this is all my fault."

I've been replaying every moment of what happened with Ivy and me in my head. If it wasn't Gemma, it would've been something else.

I wrap an arm around Gemma's shoulders, giving her a quick hug. No need to get overly sappy backstage at a music fest. "It wasn't. She was always going to find a reason to leave."

As much as I wish it weren't true, it is.

"Maybe she'll come back." Something washes over Gemma's face. I can't pinpoint it, but it was there.

"Do you know something?"

The look I give Gemma is one that used to get her to tell me anything. It's my best big brother look.

"What would I know? I've been in LA with Blake."

"I thought you got back a few days ago?" I ask her.

"We extended our trip. Blake is still out there, so I wanted to stay with him a few extra days."

"Damn. I'm losing my touch."

"Sorry, Mason. You lost it a long time ago," Logan says from where he's sitting.

"Ouch."

"Just telling the truth."

"Jesus. You two drive me crazy somedays."

"You love us," Gemma says, poking me in the side.

"I don't know why."

Except I do. They're the reason I don't want to leave. Why I'm not packing up my life and moving to Seattle.

My life is here in Dixon. It wouldn't be fair to take Willow away from so many people who love her. Me too. I know it's a small town where most people wouldn't stop on their way through.

But I love it. The people. My family. The ranch.

I just wish Ivy loved it enough to stay.

"I'm going to go grab a beer. You guys need anything?"

They both shake their heads at me as I head over to the small bar set up at the side of the stage. Nash is the only one standing around waiting for a drink.

"How's it going?" I ask, leaning against the bar.

He blows out a breath. "Good. But stressful. I keep waiting for something to go wrong."

"Why would something go wrong?"

The bartender sets a drink down in front of him. "Anything for you?"

"I'll take an IPA, please."

"Because we're dealing with moody musicians?" Nash answers my question. "They're moodier than you."

Not him too.

"Did you all have a family meeting to discuss me? First Gemma, now you."

Nash holds his hands up in defense. "Hey, I wasn't there."

"So there was something?"

Christ. My family really is a bunch of meddlers.

"It's hard not to notice how you've been lately. Especially after the blowup at dinner."

I wince. "Not one of my finer moments, that's for sure."

Nash claps me on the shoulder. "Hey, we've all been there. It sucks."

"At least you didn't have your entire family sticking their noses in your business."

A beaming smile lights up his face. "No. But now I get to be included in your family and stick my nose in your business. It's nice not being on the receiving end."

I take a gulp of the beer that's set in front of me and glance around the backstage area, packed with musicians and journalists.

People have come from far and wide to see the lineup Nash created. It's nothing short of incredible. Who knew the scraggly kid that visited here every summer would be heading up one of the biggest festivals on this side of the Mississippi.

"I'm really proud of you, Nash."

He looks uncomfortable. "Thanks, Mason."

"I mean it." I clasp his shoulder, staring at him. "I'm glad you're back and can do what you love from here. You're a part of this family, and I love you like another brother."

Nash pulls me in for a hug. "Damn you Winchesters for always making me so emotional."

"Sorry." I clap him on the back and release him. "You might as well get used to it."

"Peter and I are here for you too, you know. I know

you're on your own and it's still a year before Willow's mom comes back, but we've got your back. Whatever you need, you or Willow, we're here."

I swallow down the emotions that are threatening to burst out of me. I've been so on edge ever since Ivy left. I hate it. I'm not used to it.

"Thanks, Nash. You better get back to doing your thing." I point to a group of people that are behind us.

Nash turns, waving at them. "My job is never done."

"Better you than me."

We part ways and I head back over to my siblings. Peter is now there.

"Nash doing okay?" he asks.

"He's doing fine. You both are."

Peter is beaming as the band switches to a slow song. The lights in the crowd get low. It makes the ache in my chest even stronger.

Maybe one day. Maybe one day I'll get something like what they're writing this song about.

It just won't be with Ivy Connors.

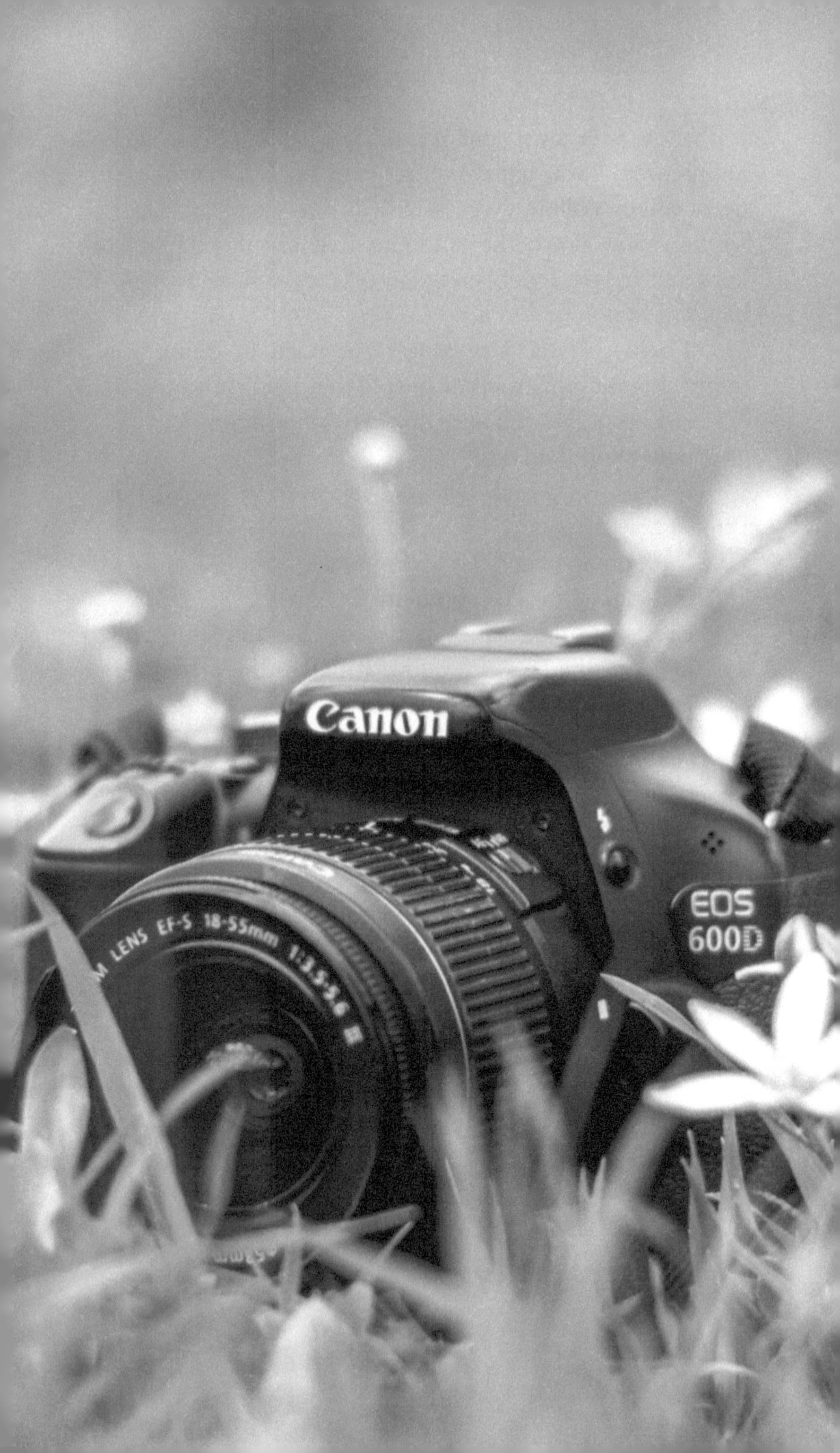
Canon
EOS
600D
LENS EF-S 18-55mm 1:3.5-5.6

Chapter Twenty-Eight

IVY

"A little to the left."

"You didn't like it there."

"It doesn't look right there either." I focus on *Summer Nights in Bloom*. It's going to be the main focal piece of the new gallery Sasha is opening.

One that she wants to have open by next Friday.

"Are you going to just stand there and look at this, or let us hang it?" the mover asks.

"Set it down."

"Can you still not decide where to hang it?" Gemma shoulders her way into the gallery, two coffees in hand.

"It doesn't feel right." I grab the coffee from her hand, sucking back half of it in one gulp.

"I thought it was good where it was."

I link my arm through Gemma's and pull her close. "It can't be good. Everything has to be perfect. I don't want to fail."

"You're Ivy Connors. You don't know how to fail."

I rest my head on her shoulder. "But what if I do?"

"Sasha wouldn't have picked you if she didn't think

you could do this. There is no one better for this job than you."

Tears well in my eyes. I've never been a big crier, but now it seems my emotions are on a hair trigger. "It feels weird being back here and not seeing them."

Gemma shifts, looking me directly in the eyes. She's got a fight in them that I don't usually see. She can be scary when she wants to be.

"Why haven't you?"

My gaze shifts to the floor. I stare at my feet. "Because I'm embarrassed."

"Why?"

"Because I left town without telling them. I tucked tail and ran and didn't look back."

Gemma laughs, looking around the small studio. "Who would've thought you'd end back up in Dixon?"

I join her, laughing what feels like the first real laugh since I got back. "Not me."

"You'll be happy here, won't you?" Gemma's voice gets quiet. "You won't want to leave in a few years?"

It's the thought I keep coming back to. Will I be happy? I wanted to live in the city, not Dixon. Travel the world. See what it has to offer outside our small town.

"Honestly? I hated being in Seattle. I thought it would be what I wanted, but it isn't."

"Do you think you'd like it over time?"

I shake my head. "I always thought I'd be untethered. Have a new man in every different city I visited."

"And now you want one man in one small town?" Gemma quirks a brow in my direction. "Even though I don't want to know anything about your relationship."

"God help me, but I do."

"You and Mason better get your shit together."

I sip the rest of my drink. "Or?"

"Or I'm going to knock some sense into both of you. It's about damn time you officially become my sister."

I give her a playful roll of my eyes. "Does that mean I get to come to family dinner?"

"You're ready. You can handle Mason, so nothing can scare you off."

The bell above the door chimes. Turning, I expect to see one of the movers, ready to hang the rest of the portraits.

"Willow?"

Willow's face is nothing short of shocked. Her mouth hangs open as she stares back at me. Layla is standing behind her, holding her backpack.

"Ivy? What are you doing here?"

I shrug a shoulder. "I'm supposed to be working."

"But I thought you moved to Seattle?"

"Turns out I missed Dixon too much."

Willow rushes to me, wrapping her arms around my waist. The tears that were on the brink earlier start to fall.

Did I miss Mason? More than I ever could have imagined. But I missed Willow just as much.

I didn't just fall for Mason. I fell for Willow too.

Mason wasn't the only pull to come back to Dixon. I wanted to be here for both of them. I want to be a part of their family.

Layla hands Gemma Willow's backpack, and they exchange a few words before Layla leaves.

"Why'd you leave?" Willow's voice is quiet as she turns to look at me. Tears slide down her face. "Were you mad at me?"

I sink down to the floor, pulling her into my lap. "I could never be mad at you." I brush a lock out of her face. "I missed you so much, Willow."

"I missed you too, Ivy." She burrows into my hold, and

I squeeze her even tighter. I don't know how I thought I could ever stay away.

"Are you going to leave again?" she asks.

I shake my head. "Not if I can help it."

"Are you going to take pictures?"

"I am. And I'm going to sell them here too."

"Does that mean you'll hang out with me during the day?" she asks.

"That depends on your dad."

Willow snickers. "Daddy is really grumpy."

My ears perk up. "He is?"

She nods, twisting in my lap to stare at me. Those big brown eyes are ready to tell me everything. "He yelled at everyone at dinner last week and didn't let me have ice cream. Even though he said he would."

"Maybe I can take you for ice cream."

"Can we go right now?" Her whole face lights up.

I look around. Gemma is waiting outside, talking on her phone. Layla is nowhere to be found.

"What were you going to do with Aunt Layla?"

Willow shrugs a shoulder. "She picked me up from school and we were going to go to her house."

"And isn't your dad going to wonder where you are?"

She shrugs another shoulder. "He says he has daddy-dar."

"Daddy-dar?" I ask.

Willow looks at me like I'm an idiot. God, I've missed this sweet girl. "He says he always knows where I am."

"Daddies are good like that."

It doesn't surprise me Mason tells her this. It's Dixon. Every person in Dixon knows the Winchesters. We look out for each other.

It's something I missed more than I ever could have realized when living in Seattle. I never met my neighbors once. No matter how many times I went to the coffee shop around the corner, I was another faceless name to them.

Hell, I even missed all the old biddies. Within an hour of being home in Dixon, I had two pies at my door, delivered with a knowing smile, like they knew I'd be back.

The door chimes again. Willow's eyes focus on the person behind her. Based on her reaction, I know exactly who it is.

Never mind the fact that my entire body starts buzzing. Weeks went by without Mason. Without his touch. Without his smile directed at me. Without him.

I missed it. More than I ever thought possible.

Being in the same room with him now brings back every feeling I thought would just be temporary.

Joke's on me though. Because the man behind me could never have been temporary.

"What in the hell are you doing here, Ivy?"

Chapter Twenty-Nine

MASON

"I thought you said you fixed this." I hold up the can as it is—a dog holding a beer in front of some mountains on the first cans of The Clara.

"Are you fucking kidding me?" Peter growls, ripping the can out from my hand. "This was not the design we agreed on."

"You sent me home before I could deal with it," I tell him matter-of-factly.

"Don't yell at me. I didn't print them." He shoves it back at my chest. "Tomorrow is bottling day, so I have to focus on that."

I clap him on the shoulder. "I can handle this. Can we at least try them?"

"What, and tell them exactly two of them popped open?" Peter looks more annoyed than usual.

I crack the can open with a hiss. "Hey, why not? Quality control." I take a big gulp; it's warm, but exactly how the Clara tastes. "Damn. That's good."

Peter grabs the can from me and takes his own sip. "Oh shit. That's refreshing."

"I told you this would be a good thing."

Rolling his eyes at me, Peter kicks back another sip. "Yeah, yeah. Don't be a know-it-all."

"Aww, look. My two brothers actually getting along," Layla's voice rings out through the quiet bar. Being three in the afternoon, we only have a few people sitting at the bar, Nash tending to them.

My gaze focuses on what's missing from Layla. "Did you forget you were supposed to pick up my daughter from school?"

"I knew I was forgetting something." Her voice is even, but her face is telling me I'm a dumbass.

"Then where is Willow?" I cross my arms. I used to be able to stare her down and she'd tell me anything. Now, it's not as easy.

"You know the old souvenir shop?"

"You left her there by herself?"

Layla rolls her eyes. "Yes, Mason. I left Willow there all by herself. Figured she'd be fine with a bucket of ice cream."

"Jesus, Layla. Where is she?"

"She's with Gemma. There was something she wanted to see, so I left the two of them together."

I blow out a breath. Logically, I knew she was fine. But it still sets my mind at ease knowing she's with my sister.

"Why don't you go check on her?" Layla asks.

"Do you not see that I'm busy?" I wave my hand in front of all the fucked-up cans of Peter's greatest creation. With them screwing it up, it hopefully will be a fast fix.

"You were so concerned about Willow, I only figured you'd want to check on her."

"Are you trying to get me out of here?"

"Layla, can you not see we're busy?" Peter tells her.

"Life isn't all about work."

"Wow." Peter and I say at the same time.

"Why are you two looking at me like that?" Layla switches her gaze between the two of us.

"Because you work more than I do," Peter says.

"And I can't pull Peter away from the bar." Nash drops a kiss on his cheek as he walks by.

"That's because you two work together and it doesn't matter," I say.

"Hey, I've been home more lately," Peter argues. "Logan needs me."

"Stop getting distracted. Mason, go get Willow."

"Fine. I'll deal with this when we get back," I tell Peter.

Downtown Dixon is bustling as I jog across the street from the bar to find Gemma standing outside one of the old shops. It's been vacant for months. I know Layla was trying to get it, but her shithead ex didn't budge.

"I thought you were supposed to be watching Willow?" Gemma is standing in front of the store. Craft paper lines the inside of the windows. Whatever is going on, this place looks like it'll be given new life soon.

Exactly what we need in Dixon. The more business we bring in, the better it is for the town.

"She's inside. Why don't you go check on her?"

I eye her. Gemma is buzzing with excitement. I'd say it's a change from the last time I saw her, but she's been like this ever since Blake moved back.

"What's with you and Layla?"

"God, nothing! Just go inside!" Gemma shoves me toward the open door, and I stop dead in my tracks. Willow's eyes find me immediately, but it's the woman she's sitting with that draws my attention.

Ivy.

Ivy fucking Connors.

The woman who has consumed my every waking

thought for the last few weeks. I haven't seen her since she walked out of that hospital waiting room. Taking my heart, and Willow's too for that matter, with her.

Willow is looking at her like she hung the moon.

"What in the hell are you doing here, Ivy?"

Fuck. I didn't mean to growl. It's like I've lost all common sense.

"Daddy, language!"

Willow is happier than I've seen her in weeks. It's like when Ivy left, she took all the joy from our house. I never realized how much impact she had on our lives. Now that she's here? I never want her to leave again.

"Willow, what have I said about that?"

She huffs. "Adults are allowed to say it. I can't because I get put in time-out at school." She turns her attention to Ivy. "Mark was making fun of me last week because I was sad, and I told him to go to hell."

"He did not!" Ivy responds.

Willow nods, her curls bouncing up and down. "And then I got in trouble because I said a not nice word."

"Maybe next time you can try ignoring him."

Willow hugs Ivy. "I'm glad you're here."

Fuck. Seeing Willow hug Ivy tugs at every heartstring I have. I don't know who's missed Ivy more—me or Willow.

"Am I interrupting this conversation?" As much as I want Willow to have this moment with Ivy, I need to talk to her.

"Daddy, I have so much to tell Ivy!" Willow admonishes me. Nothing like a seven-year-old to put you in your place.

I take a step farther into the shop. "How about you go with Aunt Gemma right now, and then I'll pick up pizza and we can have dinner with Ivy and you can tell her everything that happened at school?"

"Pepperoni with onions and hot sauce?"

"Yes, you little weirdo."

Willow runs over to me. "Thanks, Daddy." She crooks her finger at me. I bend down closer to her.

"What is it, Pipsqueak?"

"Be nice to Ivy. I really want her to stay."

"You do, do you?"

She nods. "I know you love her, Daddy."

Her words hit me square in the chest. And here I thought I did a good job hiding it. I guess she heard my outburst at dinner.

"I love her too. And I want her to stay and love us too." Willow pops a kiss on my cheek and runs out the door to meet Gemma. I watch her take her hand and they walk out of view.

Blowing out a breath, I turn to face the woman who is now giving me all of her attention. Her hands are fidgeting in front of her.

This Ivy is so different from the one I'm used to.

Gone is all that confidence that carried her into any room. I can feel her nerves from here.

"You left."

Tears well in her eyes. "I did."

"Why?"

She picks at a fingernail. "Because I screwed everything up."

I close the distance between the two of us. The second I have my arms around her, it's like everything inside my chest settles. I've been at war with myself these last few weeks. Missing her one minute and then trying to put her behind me the next.

"What'd you screw up?"

Ivy's hands land on my biceps, like she's still trying to

keep me at bay. "I lied to Gemma. I lied to you. I lied to myself."

"And these lies were?"

Ivy's blue eyes are wet, and I don't stop to think. I wipe the first signs of a tear from her cheek. I don't want this woman to feel an ounce of pain.

"I didn't tell Gemma about us, and she's the closest thing I have to a sister."

"She seemed okay to me." I continue stroking her cheek.

"We're okay now, but I never should have done it to begin with. I couldn't face you after everything happened, so I left. I figured it'd be easier for everyone if I wasn't here."

"That is the furthest thing from the truth. Fuck, we've been a mess without you."

"We?"

I nod. "You saw Willow. I don't know who missed you more."

Ivy's laugh is watery. "I screwed up, Mason. I got scared of my feelings for you and ran. I thought if I lied to myself and told myself it was just a fling, I'd be able to move on."

"Did that work?"

She shakes her head.

"I guess we were both lying to ourselves."

"What were you lying about?"

I drop my forehead to hers. "I fucking fell in love with you, Ivy. I kept telling emyself it was just for the summer. That you were convenient because you were there. It was anything but convenient."

"You love me?" Ivy's warm breath ghosts over my lips.

God. I love this woman with every ounce of my being. I never want to let her leave.

"You were never a fling, Ivy. Never temporary. You are everything to me. To us. And I want to spend the rest of my life showing you if you'll have me. And if we have to do long distance for a while, I can suck it up."

Ivy answers with a searing kiss. Her mouth on mine has every part of my body wanting to be as close as possible to her. Heat courses through my veins as she slides her tongue into my mouth.

I forgot how good it was to kiss her.

It's like Ivy Connors was made for me. Every bit of her fits perfectly with me. All too soon, she's ending the kiss. We have a few hours before I promised Willow we'd be home, and I want to make use of every second of them.

"We don't have to do long distance at all." Ivy smiles against my lips.

"What do you mean?"

Ivy's smile hits me square in the chest. And a little lower, to be perfectly honest.

"Would you believe I met someone at the gallery in Seattle that was opening one here?"

"Wait, you're not going back?"

Ivy shakes her head. "Turns out I hate city living."

"I thought you wanted to travel?"

"Sasha is going to send me to buy art wherever she finds a piece. I get to fill my travel bug but come home to Dixon."

"Say that again."

Ivy smiles, linking her hands behind my head. "I'll be coming home to Dixon. To You. To Willow."

"Those are the sweetest words I've ever heard, Ivy. I love you."

"I love you too, Mason. I never thought I'd want to live here in Dixon, but you're all I want. A life with you and Willow."

I brush the hair back from her face. "Thank you for loving my daughter so much."

"She makes it really easy."

"She'll be happy to hear you're staying. She missed you."

"God, I missed her too. I missed you both."

I growl. "Fuck, I was driving everyone crazy with how much I missed you."

"How much?" Ivy lines her entire body up with me.

Oh, yeah. My girl is back and I want to take her.

Right here. Right now. I don't want to waste any time going back to my house. Hauling her into my arms, I back us against the wall.

"Is there a place we can take this that is more private?" I nip at the tender skin on her neck. She's just as sweet as I remember.

"Office. Back hallway." Ivy's voice is breathless.

Ivy's lips come down on my neck as I walk us in the direction she told me. There's a small office, boxes littered across the floor. A desk takes up the rest of the room with a small love seat behind it.

Perfect. Just what we need.

Setting Ivy down on the small couch, I take her in. There is nothing but love shining out of her eyes. I don't know how I ever convinced myself this thing with her would only be for the summer.

I love her. Everything about her calls to me in a way I never knew. The way she loves Willow. The way she loves me. The way she completely changed her life and will now be in ours every single day.

"You're thinking pretty hard up there." Ivy starts unbuttoning her blouse. Slowly revealing those perfect tits of hers that I love so much.

Kneeling down, I spread her legs apart and pull her to

the edge of the couch. Her eyes go wide as I slide my hands up her legs, rubbing my thumbs over her core. "Thinking about how much I missed you. And how I can't wait to get inside you again."

Grabbing my wallet, I pull out a condom before we get too far into this. Ivy stops my hand. "No condom."

I eye her. "You sure? All my tests were negative the last time I got checked."

She nods. "Mine too. And I'm on the pill." Linking her hands behind my head, she pulls me closer to her. "I want to feel every bare inch of you inside me."

Fuck me. It's like my dick knows exactly what is going to happen and wants to get in on the action.

My answer is to crush my lips against hers. Every nip, every suck, every tease, reseals the connection between the two of us that I thought was broken.

Each slide of her tongue against mine is making me desperate to get inside her. I rip my mouth from hers.

Swollen lips.

Lust-filled eyes.

Blush creeping up her cheeks.

I can't wait to see how she looks once I'm inside her again.

"Why'd you stop?"

"Because I don't want to come in my pants like some chump. And you're going to make me come just from kissing you."

Ivy looks quite proud of herself as she sits up and shrugs out of her shirt. "Then you better get a move on, Mason. Because I want that cock of yours inside me. Now."

Leaning forward, I bury my face in her cleavage. My fingers pinch her nipple through the thin fabric of her bra.

"I've missed your hands." Ivy's fingers dig into my scalp, fisting the hair. Oh yeah, she definitely has.

"And I've missed these." I pull a cup of her bra down, her breast popping out. Her nipples are already hard. I play with the barbell there, knowing exactly how she likes it. Each twist and flick of my tongue, pulling the cool metal against my tongue, has Ivy writhing beneath me.

"I forgot how good you are at this." Ivy's fingers—if possible—tighten even further in my hair. The slightest sting of pain shoots straight to my leaking cock.

"I will reacquaint you however often you need, Ivy." I turn my attention to the other neglected nipple. I pull at it with my teeth, licking the sting away with my tongue.

"I am so close to coming, Mason. Oh my God!"

Ivy throws a leg over my shoulder, holding me to her. Her heel digs into my back. I pull off her.

"What are you doing?" she whines. An arm is thrown over her her eyes.

"I want you to come on my tongue." Popping open the button on her pants, I pull the zipper down. I press kiss after kiss onto her stomach as I tug her pants and underwear down. Ivy's wet and waiting for me.

I blow a warm breath over her pussy.

"You're making me crazy."

"Good." I bite at the tender skin of her thigh. "A little taste of how you've made me feel the last few weeks. I should make you wait."

Pulling back, I keep a hand on her, my touch light.

"Are you really going to keep me waiting right now?" Ivy throws her hand down. A fighting look spreads across her face.

"I should. Give you a little taste of what I went through."

Ivy strokes a hand down my cheek. It's a soft touch.

But one I want to feel everywhere. "Maybe you could do that the next time?"

Grabbing the globes of her ass, I pull her back to the edge of the couch. Her pussy is ripe for the taking. I drag my tongue through her folds, eating up every drop of her wetness. Enjoying the moans slipping from her lips.

"I guess we can save the spanking for next time."

Ivy's thighs squeeze my head as I delve my tongue inside her wet heat. I have to squeeze my own dick to keep from exploding. She tastes so damn good, I'm losing my mind. My tongue is driving inside her faster. Dragging her wetness up to her clit as I flick the tiny bundle of nerves.

I swipe my tongue each time, from inside her to her clit. It doesn't take much before she's coming on my tongue. I lap it up, drinking up every last drop of her release.

"You taste even better than I remember." I drop a wet kiss onto her lips.

"Mmm."

Reaching into my pants, I take out my leaking cock. I don't give Ivy a moment to recover before I'm pushing inside her.

"Fuck, do you ever feel amazing." She's squeezing my cock to within an inch of its life.

I take my time with her, rocking in and out in long, slow strokes. I never thought I'd get this again. Every sound she makes, I eat up.

This woman is everything I want.

It doesn't take her long to come again, dragging my own release out of me.

It feels even better knowing there is nothing between us. That it'll be the two of us together from now on.

Cum drips out of her pussy as I pull out. It's so fucking hot seeing her like this, my seed inside of her. It's something I want to see every damn day for the rest of my life. Knowing this gorgeous woman is mine and only mine.

Fuck, it's so damn hot. I'm boneless, shifting onto the couch and pulling Ivy into my lap.

"That's even better than I remember." Her small hands roam over my chest.

"I'll remind you as often as you need me to. As long as it means you're staying here."

Glancing up at me, Ivy's eyes are soft. She's completely blissed out.

"I guess I just needed someone to show me this small town was worth it."

I tuck a lock of hair behind her ear. "It is. We are. And I'll remind you of that any time you need me to."

Ivy laughs in my arms.

"What's so funny?"

"It's just, I remember hating this town so much. People always being so nosy, wanting to set me up with someone. I guess the joke's on me."

I kiss her hair. "I guess that's just the way this small town works."

"And I couldn't love Dixon more for it."

Canon
EOS
600D
M LENS EF-S 18-55mm 1:3.5-5.6

"Ivy, are you almost ready?" Mason calls out to me.

"We're not in a hurry." Grabbing a tank top out of my suitcase, I pull it down over my swimsuit.

With only a few short weeks left in summer, and Willow going to visit her mom now that she's back stateside, we wanted one more trip together with the three of us.

Sasha found a landscape of the Smokies she wanted in a small town in Tennessee, so we all came out here together.

After exploring the town, we're heading out to find the waterfalls we've heard so much about that are in the area.

Willow comes running upstairs as I grab my backpack to go down.

"Did your dad send you up here?"

She nods, pigtails bouncing. "He said you're taking too long."

"Waterfalls aren't going anywhere, Willow." Grabbing her shoulders and turning her, we head downstairs. Mason is pacing in the small living room of our cabin.

It's full of dark wood and stained glass windows. It's

the complete opposite of the cabins at the ranch back home. But I've loved every minute we've spent here this week.

Mason stops when he sees us, a small smile playing on his lips. "Finally ready?"

I saunter over to him, wrapping my arms around his waist. "Why are you in such a hurry?"

"I don't want to lose the sunlight."

"Last I checked, we have all afternoon."

"Such a smart-ass." Mason drops a quick kiss on my lips.

Willow groans behind us. "You kiss too much."

"Then close your eyes, kid."

Mason drops another kiss on my lips.

Every time he kisses me feels like the first time. The butterflies. The tingles down my spine. I never want to lose this feeling with Mason.

All too soon, Mason is pulling back. "We should probably get going."

"Yes!" Willow calls out behind us. "I want to find the waterfalls."

Willow is ready, backpack on and hiking boots all tied up.

"Let's go." Mason grabs my hand as Willow runs out the door ahead of us.

The trailhead is behind the cabins here outside of town. It's an easy hike through the foothills, nothing we don't do at home on the weekends.

Crunched up leaves line the wide trail as Willow has her camera out, taking pictures of everything she sees.

"This is nice." Mason wraps an arm around my shoulders, pulling me into his side.

"Exactly where I want to be."

It's hard to believe this is my life. I was able to bring

two of my favorite people with me to this small town. And when we're done here, we're going home to Dixon.

No other place I'd rather be.

"Ivy! Look how cool this is!" Willow runs back up to us, holding her camera out.

I bought myself a new one after the big opening in Dixon and gave Willow my old one. I love that she shares my passion for it.

A wildflower fills the screen while everything behind it is out of focus.

"That's beautiful, Willow."

"Can we print it when we get home?"

"Of course."

She runs back up the trail.

"I love how much she loves photography because of you."

I smile, linking hands now with Mason as the sound of waterfalls draws us farther into the trees. Even though it's the middle of summer, we have the trail to ourselves. I like that it's just the three of us out here.

"Are you sick of all of her pictures covering the wall?"

"Not at all. I love it."

Instead of her paintings, now her photos—mostly the mountains, flowers and Daisy—cover the walls of our house.

Our house.

While I stayed at my studio apartment in town for a few months, I spent most free nights at Mason's. We made it official this past spring.

I let out a sigh. "I'm going to miss her."

Mason squeezes me closer to him. "Don't remind me. I know it'll only be a few weeks before school starts, but I'm already dreading it."

Leaning up, I nip at Mason's jaw. "Maybe I can do

something to take your mind off it."

Mason growls. "Damn it, Ivy. Not now. We can't do anything here."

"Giving you a preview of later." Patting his chest, I run up the path toward Willow.

Willow is pointing around the curve in the trail. "I found the waterfall."

The roar is louder up here as the path spits us out at a small waterfall. Rocks line the plunge pool. A rainbow cuts through the mist.

It's a little slice of heaven. Only for us. We're the only people out here.

"Wow."

Willow's got her camera out, snapping pictures.

"Holy shit," Mason breathes behind me. "They weren't kidding about this place."

I grab my own camera and take pictures myself. I want to remember every bit of this trip. As I'm snapping pictures, Mason runs through the viewfinder, jumping into the water.

"Damn, that feels good."

Willow sets her stuff down and follows her dad into the water.

"Are you coming, Ivy?" she asks when she pops up from the water. Her eyes are bright and happy.

"Give me a minute."

Willow swims over to Mason, leaping into his waiting arms. I snap a photo before getting down to my swimsuit and jumping in.

The water is ice-cold. It's like icicles are sticking to my skin.

"It's freezing." I wipe the water from my eyes.

"I want to try a cannonball," Willow says, swimming over to the rocks.

"Be careful!" I call after her.

"You worry too much," Mason says, swimming up to me.

"Please."

Except I know I do. I love that little girl something fierce and worry more than I should. As Mason likes to point out every chance he can get.

Every day I get to spend with her makes me want my own little one with Mason.

Willow steadies herself on the rock before launching herself into the swimming hole, tucking her legs up and splashing in the water.

"Ten out of ten!" Mason shouts behind me as she pops up and swims over to us. "Think you can do better, Ivy?"

"What? Since when did this become a contest?"

"I think my cannonball is the best." There's a fierce determination in her eyes.

"Let's prove it," Mason eggs us on.

I quirk a brow in Mason's direction. "Oh really? You plan on joining us?"

A panicked look washes over his face. "Oh, hell no. You think I can do a cannonball? No way. I'd break myself in two."

"You can be the judge, then." I swim after Willow, both of us heading over to the rock where Willow jumped the first time.

"Are you really going to pit me against you two?" He crosses his arms, chest glinting in the sunlight. Mason is every bit as handsome now as when I first noticed him.

A rainbow of color floats behind him from the water-fall. It's the perfect ending to our day of exploring before we head back into town.

I don't know how there aren't more people here, but I'm grateful it's just us. It's one of the few times a year that the three of us can travel together. With Willow out of school and things not quite as busy in Dixon, we're able to mix family time with a bit of work for me.

Not that taking pictures out here is work.

It's the best of both worlds. Filling my need to travel while having Mason and Willow at my side.

"Dad, you have to be fair."

"Fine. But I'm doing this out of protest," Mason grumbles. "You first, Willow."

"Yes!" She pumps her fist and finds a good spot on the rock. Mason winks at me from his spot near the waterfall.

God, I love this man.

Willow takes a running leap and flies into the water, splashing all of us. She comes up sputtering, swimming over to Mason.

"That'll be hard to beat, Pipsqueak."

"Dad, I'm not Pipsqueak anymore."

I can feel her eye roll from here, even though her back is to me. I still remember the day she came home from school and started calling Mason Dad. Said all the kids at school call their parents Mom and Dad. About broke his heart.

"Sorry, Willow." A small smile plays on his lips. "You're up, Ivy."

I take off and tuck my legs up as the water comes up to meet me. It's just as cold going into the water this time as it was the first.

"Alright." I wipe the water out of my eyes. "Who's the winner?"

"Me. I had more splash." Willow is adamant.

"How would you know? You didn't see it." I swim over to the two of them.

Mason groans. "Can we call it a tie?"

"You have to pick a winner!" Willow and I shout at the

same time, causing us both to start laughing.

"I'm getting my sandwich. I don't want to be in the middle of you two." I don't miss the smile on his face as he gets out of the water.

"What a chicken," I tell him.

"Yeah, you're a chicken, Dad."

"Are you two going to gang up on me all vacation?"

"Yes," we both tell him again.

"Ivy. Will you help me take a picture?" Willow follows Mason out of the water. They exchange a look, but Mason goes back to digging in his bag for the lunch we packed.

"Of course."

It's warmer out of the water. The sun breaks through, heating my skin.

It really is the perfect day.

"I'm ready, Ivy."

I turn, but what I see is the last thing I expect.

Mason is down on one knee, Willow standing beside him with her hands clasped under her chin.

"What's going on?" I blurt out.

Way to go, Ivy.

It's pretty obvious what's going on.

Mason is down on one knee.

"I hope it's fairly clear what I'm going to do."

"Oh my God."

"Mind coming over here?" Mason cocks an eyebrow at me.

I step closer, grabbing his hand that he holds out for me.

"Ivy Connors. You are absolutely the love of my life. I never thought I would get so lucky to love someone like you."

Tears gather in my eyes.

"The love you show me and Willow is something I'll

never take for granted. I want days like this. I want to travel with you. I want to spend our days in Dixon. At the bar. As long as I get to spend every single day of my life with you, I'll be a happy, happy man."

My vision blurs. Willow is bouncing with excitement next to him.

"Ivy Connors. Will you marry me?"

The box he pops open holds an antique ring. The oval-cut diamond sits on a thin white gold band. "Oh my God, it's beautiful."

Mason rubs a thumb over my ring finger. "It was my grandma's."

You could see my smile from space, it's so big.

"Ye—"

Willow cuts me off.

"Please, please, *please* say yes, Ivy!" Willow's hands are clasped under her chin, eyes wide with excitement.

I don't know how I could ever say no to her.

Or the man down on one knee for me.

"Yes! Of course!" Both of them wrap me in a hug as Mason plants one on my lips.

"Thank God," Mason whispers against my lips.

"I don't know why you were so worried. You know I can't ever say no to you."

"I have something for you too!" Willow chirps.

"As long as I have you two, I have everything I need."

My voice is still shaky. Mason and I talked about marriage, but it always seemed like such a faraway thing. But with the bar doing well and the gallery taking off, I don't really know why we were waiting.

Mason wasn't, apparently.

"Are you surprised?"

"No wonder you were so antsy to get going."

Mason laughs, his breath warm on my face. "I've

chickened out like three times this week."

"That doesn't sound like you."

"Hey, it's nerve-racking."

Willow comes back, handing me a small black box. I pop open the lid to find a small gold willow branch charm sitting on the velvet.

As if I wasn't already crying before, the tears fall harder. "I love it." I pull her in for a hug.

"I can't wait for you to be my stepmom."

I kiss Willow's cheek. "I love you so much. So much, I might even let you win the next cannonball contest."

"Yes!" Her sweet laugh rings through the small area.

How did I get so lucky?

I never pictured this would be my life. Paris. Tokyo. Sydney. You name it, I wanted to live in any city I could find on the map that wasn't Dixon. Everything I wanted was outside the town I grew up in.

Now? Now, everything is in Dixon.

Mason. Willow. Gemma. The gallery.

My entire life is Dixon and I wouldn't have it any other way.

Mason wipes a tear away from my cheek as I stare into the face I love so much.

"What's going on in that head of yours?"

I smile, still holding Willow in my arms.

"Who knew I would love Dixon so much?"

THE END

KEEP READING for a special bonus scene with Mason, Ivy and Willow…

Bonus Scene

MASON

"Can I have one more piece? Please?"

"You've already had two pieces, Pipsqueak."

"But I'm hungry!" Willow whines.

"Let her have another piece," Ivy tells me.

"Ivy said yes." Willow ignores me and grabs the last piece of pizza from the box. Covering the pepperoni's and onions with hot sauce, she takes a huge bite.

"Can you take smaller bites, Willow? I don't want you choking on dinner." I quirk my brow at her.

"Sorry." She eyes me then Ivy, before diving back into her food.

"Is all this hot sauce good for her and her tonsils?" Ivy asks, taking a much smaller bite of her own pizza.

"She's okay. Had more ice cream than she knew what to do with, though."

Willow swallows her bite. "Daddy says I can't eat any more ice cream because I ate all of it in Dixon."

Ivy laughs. "You probably did."

"Is there any for dessert?" Willow asks.

"Not tonight. Maybe tomorrow."

"Yes!" Willow pumps her arm. "Ivy can make sundaes with us."

"We can do whatever you want." She wraps my daughter up in a side hug. "I'm not going anywhere."

Willow doesn't see it, but I do, the softness that washes over her as she hugs my daughter. The love Ivy has for her–when she isn't her own daughter–blows me away. This woman is incredible and I really don't know how I got so lucky.

"Does that mean Ivy is going to live with us now?" Willow asks.

"Umm…" Ivy's eyes go wide.

"We haven't talked about that yet," I tell her. "That's a conversation for adults."

"She can share my room." She ignores me.

The look of excitement on my daughter's face warms my heart. Dealing with a sad kid is never something any parent wants to deal with. And Willow missing Ivy? It was almost more than I could bear.

"We'll see." I throw the empty pizza box into the trash. "It's time to get ready for bed."

"But Ivy just got here!"

"Sorry, Pipsqueak. It's a school night."

"Can Ivy read me a story?" Willow hops off the stool, coming over to me to plead her case.

I drop a kiss on her head. "As long as I get to listen."

Her head nods in excitement. "Yes!"

"Okay, go brush your teeth and we'll be in there in a minute."

Willow darts toward her room, Daisy hot on her heels.

My gaze darts back to Ivy. I haven't had enough time with her yet. As soon as we left her studio, we picked up dinner and came straight home. As much as I missed her, so did Willow. I couldn't deny my daughter getting time with Ivy.

"Why do you keep looking at me like that?" Ivy breaks me from my thoughts.

"Like what?"

"Like you're afraid I'm going to disappear."

Stepping around the bar, I grab her thighs and spread them, stepping between her legs. "It's hard to believe you're here."

Ivy's eyes get glassy. "I'm sorry I ever left."

"Don't be." I drop my forehead to hers. "You came back."

Her eyes flutter close as she sucks in a deep breath. "I love you Mason. And Willow. This is where I want to be. For as long as you'll have me."

"Oh yeah?" I cup her cheeks, brushing my thumbs over her cheeks. "I know what I want. I love you, Ivy, and so does my daughter. And we want you here. I don't want to waste any time. Move in with us. Join our family."

"My childhood dream might just be coming true then."

"What dream is that?"

"Getting to be a Winchester."

"Fuck." My dick grows hard in my pants at hearing her say that. "Do you know what that does to me?"

A small smile plays at her lips. "I can guess. About the same thing to me. Knowing that I'll always be yours."

"I love you." I go in for a kiss, but her fingers on my lips stop me. "What?" I mumble.

"I have one condition to move in."

"What's that?"

"Do you think Willow and I could get bunk beds?"

Wrapping my arm around her waist, I pull her to me. "The only bed you'll be sharing is with me."

"Promise?"

I slant my mouth over hers in the best kiss of my life. Fuck, do I ever love this woman. Each stroke of her tongue against mine has me wanting to drag her back to my room and relearn her body. I don't give a shit if I was just with her a few hours ago. Ivy is my drug that I will never get enough of.

"Are you going to do that a lot more now?" Willow bursts into the kitchen, now in her t-shirt and sleep shorts.

I jump away from Ivy. A blush creeps up Ivy's cheeks.

Busted.

"We'll try to keep the kissing to a minimum." Although, with Ivy living here now, we might need to set some new ground rules.

Because if I have my say? I'm going to be buried deep inside the woman I love every night.

Ivy winks at me as she gets dragged back to Willow's room. I clean the kitchen, not wanting to mess with it tomorrow. Tomorrow, I'm taking my girls out to breakfast.

My girls.

I don't know if I'll ever get tired of saying that. Throwing the dish towel into the sink, I follow the sound of laughter to the other side of the house.

The picture as I walk into Willow's room hits me straight in the gut. Sure, Ivy read Willow books before, but something about this time makes my chest swell.

Ivy, holding one of Willow's favorite books, is leaning against the headboard with Willow tucked into her side.

This is something we'll get to do every night. Together.

I finally have someone I can lean on. My daughter is the most special person in my world, and I never trusted anyone with her. Turns out, I was just waiting for Ivy. Someone to realize just how special Willow is.

When I hired Ivy to help me with Willow, I never thought that *this* is what I would be getting. Someone who loves us unconditionally. Who will always be here for us.

A family.

I'm the luckiest bastard in the world.

Book number 14 (I think this is right?! I'm beginning to lose count…)is now out in the world!

I cannot even begin to tell you how much love I have for Mason, Ivy and Willow! I worried and stressed more than you'll ever know over this little family. They absolutely stole my heart, and I don't know if I'll ever be able to let them go! Thank you for picking up this book and thank you for loving Dixon as much as I do!

There are so many amazing author friends that have come into my life since I started this journey. I'm beyond lucky. I don't know if this book would've happened without daily sprints with Stephanie Rose and CE Johnson…you two kept me going! To Tina…the best unpaid intern out there! Let's get some Cake Bake to celebrate! And to every other author out there that has supported me on this journey…I love you and adore you and you are too many to name!

Thank you to my beta readers Jodi and Ashlee for making this book amazing! I'm so happy to have you on this journey with me. Thank you to every person that has read, reviewed, shared, created edits, TikToked…you name it, your support has been the best part of this journey. To hear how much you love my books always puts a smile on my face! To my Street Team…your support is unwavering and I never take it for granted! And my Travelers…my group is my favorite little corner of the internet!

And to all the readers…thank you for picking up my books and making my dream a reality!

<3 Emily

About the Author

After winning a Young Author's Award in second grade, Emily Silver was destined to be a writer. She loves writing inclusive stories, with strong heroines and the swoony men who fall for them.

A lover of all things romance, Emily started writing books set in her favorite places around the world. As an avid traveler, she's been to all seven continents and sailed around the globe.

When she's not writing, Emily can be found sipping cocktails on her porch, reading all the romance she can get her hands on and planning her next big adventure!

Find her on social media to stay up to date on all her adventures and upcoming releases!

The Love Abroad Series

An Icy Infatuation

A French Fling

A Sydney Surprise

Read all my books here:

9 781961 359109